THE FIRE OF REVENGE

THE MARINE LETSCO TRILOGY
BOOK TWO

PAM B. NEWBERRY

J. K. Brooks Publishing, LLC
WYTHEVILLE, VA

Copyright © 2015 by Pam B. Newberry.

All rights reserved. No part of this publication may be reproduced, distributed or transmitted in any form or by any means, including photocopying, recording, or other electronic or mechanical methods, without the prior written permission of the publisher, except in the case of brief quotations embodied in critical reviews and certain other noncommercial uses permitted by copyright law. For permission requests, write to the J. K. Brooks Publishing, LLC, addressed "Attention: Permissions Coordinator," at the address below.

J. K. Brooks Publishing, LLC
177 Stone Meadow Lane
Wytheville, VA 24382
http://jkbrookspublishing.com

Publisher's Note: This is a work of fiction. Names, characters, places, and incidents are a product of the author's imagination. Locales and public names are sometimes used for atmospheric purposes. Any resemblance to actual people, living or dead, or to businesses, companies, events, institutions, or locales is completely coincidental.

Book Cover Design ©2015 Julie Kay Newberry
Book Layout ©2013 BookDesignTemplates.com

Ordering Information:
Quantity sales. Special discounts are available on quantity purchases by corporations, associations, and others. For details, contact the "Special Sales Department" at the address above.

The Fire of Revenge/ Pam B. Newberry. -- 1st ed.
ISBN-10: 1941061036
ISBN-13: 978-1-941061-03-9

To my daughter, I love you!

> "I could have gotten answers. I could have learned more about who I was before, and why she wanted me dead. I could have learned why it was so horribly wrong to be me."
>
> —MARINE LETSCO

ONE

HAVE YOU SEEN HER?

The New Brook Christmas parade began to make its way down the long, dark main street at six o'clock in the evening. The street was lined with children and parents. A brisk, cold winter air seemed to find crevices to seep through bringing a chill to the bones. The spectators were ready to greet Santa Claus and cheer for their favorite floats. They stomped their feet, patted glove-covered hands, and moved around in an effort to stay warm. Once the parade reached the crowd, the event sprang to life. Santa perched high on the New Brook Fire Department's ladder truck, waved while Christmas music was piped through the truck's PA system into the streets.

Sixteen well-groomed horses of various breeds followed at a proper distance. All were adorned with Christmas decorations, silver-trimmed bridles, and the riders were dressed in different costumes from elves to western wear. The regal horses' costumes were finished with brightly colored ribbons and lights woven in their manes and tails. The lights appeared to flash to the beat of the music.

Marine Letsco marveled at how well-mannered the horses were until the parade started. Then, her work began. Serving as the tail end of the parade, Rotary members, who were active citizens of the community—judges, lawyers, bank presidents, hospital executives, and local business owners—made up the Rotary parade entry lovingly called the Pooper-Scoopers. Annually, the Rotary offered this service to the community. Considered a dirty job by some, others thought it was a lighthearted end to a celebration that signaled the beginning of the Christmas season. It was their job to walk behind the horses along the parade route and scoop up the manure as it was dropped. It was then deposited into a trailer that was being pulled behind a member's John Deere Gator utility vehicle.

"I can't believe you talked me into doing this, Chet," Marine said as she shoveled a horse's lovingly deposited present. "What will Aunt Betsy do with this when we get it home?"

"You are a good sport for helping. And, yes, we will use it. We will place it in a special composting pile where we will allow it to age. Next spring, this will make an excellent supplement for the garden. Aunt Betsy has used these gifts from the horses for several years now. That is why our garden is so productive. At least, that is what she will tell you."

Marine shook her head and wondered just how much more productive a garden could be. When she first met Aunt Betsy, after arriving in New Brook eight months earlier, she marveled at all of the work that went into planning, preparing, and tending a vegetable garden. Aunt Betsy knew how to turn soil into black gold, as she called it.

The parade continued down the street. Marine looked into the faces of the people standing along the side of the street waving to Santa and even cheering the Pooper-Scoopers on as they walked along doing their chore.

Marine stopped.

"Marine, are you okay?" Chet said as he came up beside her.

Dr. Chet Henegar was Marine's doctor after she suffered a fall while on a cruise in the Caribbean. Marine had lost her memory because of that fall. Chet began to treat her with a memory recall method. When the cruise ended, Chet offered Marine a place to stay with Elizabeth James Lanter, his Aunt Betsy so that he could continue her treatment. Chet lived in his own apartment in the Southwest Virginia town of New Brook nestled in the Blue Ridge Mountains—a suburb of Evansham, a growing metropolitan area. His office, located in a cottage at the back of Aunt Betsy's Victorian home, was where Marine and Chet met. As a result, he and Aunt Betsy had become close to Marine.

"Marine?"

"Yes. Chet. I'm sorry. I'm fine. I could have sworn I just saw—no, it couldn't be."

"Who? Drake?"

"No. Not Drake. He said he wouldn't be able to attend the parade tonight."

Drake Bianchi had also befriended Marine while on the cruise. He would drop in from one of his trips for a visit every so often since she'd moved to New Brook in April.

"Who then?"

"I'm not sure, but I thought it was Ana-Geliza."

"Ana-Geliza. I have not heard her name in a while. She was your cabin steward on the cruise, right?"

"Yes. And, well, I thought she was—"

"Was what?"

"Oh, never mind. We had better catch up with the group. We are definitely the tail end of the parade now. People behind us are starting to leave and get in their cars."

During the rest of the parade, Marine kept looking into the crowd hoping that she would catch a glimpse of Ana-Geliza again. It had to be her. But how could it be, she wondered. Drake, a photographer for the cruise, had helped her the last night on the ship when she was almost killed by Ana-Geliza. He had told her Ana-Geliza would not hurt her again.

Marine thought back to that last night she was on the ship. It had been three days spent in the ship's infirmary after falling and losing my memory. Then unexpectedly, Ana-Geliza, who was my cabin steward, forced her way into my cabin that last night and attacked me. I thought I killed her. I knew I'd never forget her face as she looked at me as she fell over the balcony railing of my cabin to the deck below. How could it be her? Why was she after me?

The parade ended. It was time for Marine and Chet's job to switch from scooping poop to securing the shovels on top of the pile of horse manure they had collected, and then to get the manure back to Aunt Betsy's barn at the back of her property.

"This is a horrid job, Chet. I can't believe you talked me into doing this. The smell is so strong I can almost taste it. Yuck!"

"It is rather stinky. But, it is a service and Aunt Betsy likes having her manure."

They laughed.

"All I've got to say is I sure hope those garden veggies will appreciate our labor come spring."

They prepped the Gator in order to drive the manure to Trout House Falls, Aunt Betsy's farm.

"Marine. You seemed pre-occupied through most of the parade. Are you okay?"

"Yes, Chet. I guess I'm just so nervous about tomorrow."

"You have nothing to be nervous about. You have started a new life here. Now, you are on the verge of beginning a new career, one of service to your community, as a female firefighter. You should be proud."

"I am. But, I've got to get through that speech tomorrow."

"You will do fine. You have written a good speech and one that will highlight the importance of trusting your fellow firefighters. What are you worried about?"

"Have you ever had a feeling that something was going to change and it wasn't going to be good?" Chet nodded his head. "Well, I feel a cloud of change hanging over me."

"Change is what happens in life. The smart thing to do is to anticipate the good changes and not brood about potential bad ones. Tomorrow will be a good change for you. Come on. We need to go meet Aunt Betsy at the firehouse. I believe they have hot coffee and cakes for us. And then, we'll haul this back to the barn."

As Marine turned to walk with Chet to the firehouse on the next block, she caught a glimpse of the figure she saw earlier. She took off in the direction of where the person walked—weaving in and out of the crowd. Every now and then, Marine thought she caught another glimpse of the mysterious person. Within a few minutes of trailing the figure, she turned down a dark alleyway between two tall buildings that lead to the local park. She stopped. I shouldn't head that way without backup or at least some kind of protection. Of all the times not to have a gun. She stood there and argued with herself about the need to be safe and the desire to find out if the lone figure was Ana-Geliza.

"Marine? Marine, where are you?" Chet called for her.

"I'm here, Chet. I'm coming." She would have to wait until later to find out who it was. But it couldn't be Ana-Geliza, could it? Marine looked back over her shoulder and shook off the feeling she was being watched.

TWO

....

REVENGE LOOMING

Ana-Geliza Morrison stood five feet six inches tall, with long, flowing ebony hair. She was of mixed Anglo-Spanish descent. She hated Marine Letsco, the assassin of her brother. Ana-Geliza hated Marine enough that all she thought about was how she was going to exact her revenge. The first time she met Marine was when she was on a stakeout right after Transcontinental Solutions, or TRANS as everyone referred to the company, had hired her. TRANS was an acronym for Terminate, Reeducate, Assassinate, Neutralize, and Sabotage. It was a company employed by governments and respected government leaders, intent on enacting an assassination with no possible association with the outcome.

Ana-Geliza was in training when she learned Marine was one of the top agents for TRANS. At first, she idolized Marine and hoped one day to be considered her closest confidant.

When her brother was murdered, Ana-Geliza used her brother's contacts to find out who had ordered his hit. Soon after discovering that TRANS did contract killings for different state governments and rival businesses around the world, she used her skill and charm to position herself as a second under Marine's tutelage. It wasn't long after moving into her new position that she learned the agent in charge of her brother's assassination was Marine. Ana-Geliza then put into motion her plan for revenge.

Her brother had always been good to her in spite of what he did for a living. He was a cartel boss involved in human trafficking. Two weeks before he was killed, he had told Ana-Geliza he was secretly leaving the cartel by going into hiding as a security guard at an oil refinery. Then, Marine had taken him out.

Ana-Geliza snagged her finger as she zipped her bag. "Damn." She went on about preparing for her move. *Getting my revenge is my only* goal, she thought. It would have been all wrapped up on the Caribbean cruise, if Drake Bianchi hadn't stepped in and foiled her plans. Now, since leaving TRANS eight months ago, she had nothing to lose but time. Giving Marine what she gave her brother—death— would make this work worthwhile.

It took Ana-Geliza six months to make her way to New Brook and another month to position herself in the town so that no one was the wiser. She placed her bag into the trunk of her car as she thought back to that last night. When Drake left me in the infirmary, stealing painkillers, and then making sure no one saw me, gave me a chance to trail him. Drake was a fool. He never noticed. And Marine was even more of a fool. That last night on the ship, Marine thought she killed me. It would take a lot more than her throwing me over a balcony to do me in. The pain was excruciating, but playing possum had always served me well.

That night, after downing five painkillers, the plan for revenge was put into play. Tonight, Marine saw enough of me that it would give her pause. She had that deer-in-the-headlights look in her eyes. She definitely had a look that made me think she saw a ghost.

"I hope I scared her," Ana-Geliza spoke aloud as she backed her car out of the drive. On the drive to her new hiding place, she considered her options. Dr. Henegar and his old aunt could be the pawns needed to help me trap Marine. With her memory gone, she won't realize my next moves. Revenge will be best served cold, and oh, so sweet.

THREE

....

THE BELL TOLLS

The Evansham Regional Fire Academy auditorium was packed to capacity for the Sunday graduating ceremony of Fire Academy Class 29. The usual dignitaries were present—the mayor, district congressional representative, the city manager, members of council, and the chiefs of each of the four fire departments that made up the joint training facility. The graduating cadets had completed twelve weeks of training and represented each fire department. There were other honored guests and family members of Class 29. None of those present meant more to Marine than those sitting in the audience that she considered her family—Chet and Aunt Betsy.

Selected as The Academy Leader, Marine walked up to the podium, looked out at the guests, dignitaries, and her fellow classmates, and then began,

> Mayor Crewe, Congressman Middleton, City Manager Sutherland, Members of the City Council of New Brook, Chief Brooks, Battalion Chiefs Stephens, Henley, Seagle, and Whisman, other honored guests, and families.
>
> It is with great pride that I stand before you today, selected by my peers to serve as Evansham Regional Fire Academy Class 29 Academy Leader. The Class 29 cadets thank all of you for taking the time to be with us. It is a milestone in each of our lives. There is a rich history and tradition in the fire service. Upon the formal conclusion of the graduation ceremony, we will begin to become part of that history and tradition. As I look out over the audience, I see the faces of many of the members of the regional fire departments who have all stood here. After going through the twelve weeks of training, they share in and understand what we are feeling at this moment.
>
> These past twelve weeks have been challenging. There were moments when we fell down, or stumbled, as we learned the job. We learned how to work as a team. We learned about each other as individuals. Yet, our fellow brothers and sisters in the fire service and those we serve, you, the citizens, do not care how many times we stumbled. It was how we got up, how we moved forward,

The Fire of Revenge

and how we were resolute in learning how to preserve life, to protect property, and to promote public safety.

I realize the pursuit of fire safety isn't as glamorous or dramatic as the pursuit of fighting fire. But we have no more urgent duty before us. We have chosen an occupation that means a devotion to lifelong service. Here, before us, is the American LaFrance engine bell. It has been prominently placed on display. It is a reminder of who we are now and every time the bell tolls, it is a reminder of who we once were.

You see, when we first came to the Fire Academy, we were told the story of the bell that once rode proudly on Fire Engine 9. The bell had been placed there when Engine 9 was first commissioned. It served Engine 9 and its entire firefighter staff well. It would sound out as a call came for all firefighters to respond. On one pivotal day in 1945, the fire engine began its run to a major fire. Heedless of impending danger, the engine began to weave through traffic. A tractor-trailer came barreling down the highway, unaware of the blocked road. The collision resulted in the total destruction of Engine 9. The bell was so mangled; the only option was to have it towed along with the engine to a city lot where the pair sat for years. Over time, they were lost to the passerby, covered with weeds and brush.

Times change, people change, and no one

remembered Engine 9 wasting away in that lot. One fateful day, the city fathers decided it needed some land for a proposed regional fire academy. The land that was to be used was the lot where Engine 9 and the bell were waiting to be found. The city workers, while cleaning the area of its debris, came across the engine, at which point they called the fire department. A few firefighters were charged with determining what to do with Engine 9. After looking at the remains, they decided that it would be sold for scrap. But a young firefighter said he thought the bell could be reshaped and used again.

Have you ever wondered how a bell is forged? To have a good sounding bell, it must be cast from raw materials that have been refined. This bell had been made that way, and though mangled, when the young firefighter pulled its string, it still gave a beautiful tone. His fellow firefighters agreed. The bell should be salvaged. It was reshaped by a local craftsman and presented to the Fire Academy in honor of all those firefighters who have dedicated their lives to service.

Regardless of where we were before, we came together twelve weeks ago to form Class 29. During these weeks, we've been newly forged and reshaped by our instructors and academy officers. Like the bell from Engine 9, we were put through the refinement process of physical training, professional studies, and molded to acquire the

The Fire of Revenge

skills necessary to do the job. And, just as the bell was polished and readied for service, we, too, have been prepared.

During the training, The Bell, as it is known, is rung twice each day—once to start the day's training and once to signal the day's end. Over the course of our training here, we have heard this bell toll one hundred and twenty times. Today, you will be privileged to hear The Bell toll as it honors those who came before us as we prepare to begin our journey as certified firefighters.

It has been my honor and pleasure to serve as Academy Leader for such an outstanding group of men and women. We have grown together, worked hard, and had fun, too. Through it all, we have become a very strong class, ready for any challenge that may be thrown our way.

At this time, I would like to call forward Chief Brooks, Battalion Chiefs Stephens, Henley, Seagle, and Whisman. We have a class motto: *We were forged through fire, bound by friendship, and our service will never be broken.* This motto has been affixed to our commemorative coin that I would now like to present to you.

Thank you.

Marine's commencement speech ended with a standing ovation. As she waited for the applause to subside, she walked over to The Bell that stood on a nearby stand made of oak. It had been buffed to a supreme shine. Below it hung a plaque with the names of the firefighters who had lost their lives during their service to the fire departments in the region.

The room was quiet as Marine reached down and rang the bell with a single toll. Then, she turned to the class member closest to her and nodded. He walked up and repeated the toll. Each of the remaining twenty-four members did the same. The cadets then filed across the stage. Each was presented his or her certificate, a commemorative coin, and a fire department badge.

The cadets stood at attention as Fire Academy Captain Duncan walked up to the podium and announced, "Class 29, you are dismissed." The ceremony ended as cheers and applause erupted from the audience.

"Now, I can breathe." Marine walked down from the stage to Chet and Aunt Betsy. "I can't believe it is really over."

"You were wonderful. This was a hallmark moment for you," Aunt Betsy said as she wrapped her arms around Marine. "I'm so very proud of you." Marine smiled as she thought how lucky she was to have these folks in her life.

"Marine. I do believe you gave the best speech I have heard given by anyone in this fair city." Chet shook her hand.

"Thank you, Chet. That means a lot to me hearing you say that since you were a professor."

"He wasn't that good of a speaker. Speaking before a small group of students isn't the same thing as what you just did. You were the best in your class. How wonderful." Aunt Betsy began to put on her coat. Marine noticed a tear fall on her cheek.

"Are we ready to go?" Marine said as she handed her certificate and coin to Chet and proceeded to pin her badge on the lapel of her uniform. "How do I look?"

"You look official. You are now a firefighter for New Brook Chestnut Mountain Station Three. And, yes, we are heading over to Belle's. We are going to celebrate." Chet handed the certificate and coin back to Marine. "That coin is a special token. I heard one of your classmates say that each of you in the class are expected to keep the coin with you whenever you fight a fire."

"Yes. It's a nice tradition. The coin has the profile of St. Florian, the patron saint of the fire service with our class motto on one side and the firefighter's prayer on the other. So, why are we going to Belle's? Can't we go home and relax at the house?"

"There will be too many people to fit in our little house. All our friends want to be a part of giving you a pat on the back. So, Belle's it had to be." Aunt Betsy laced her arm through Marine's. "Come on, Chet. Let's go get some sweets."

The ride to Belle's would take at least thirty minutes. After the excitement of graduating, Marine sat in the back seat of Chet's black Chrysler 300 and looked out at the landscape. She began to think about the first time she rode with Chet into New Brook. It was almost hard to imagine that a little more than eight months before she was getting off a cruise ship and venturing into a world where she had no memory of who she was or where she would go.

FOUR

....

THERE AND BACK AGAIN

Marine reached down and pulled her journal from her leather bag. She had made a habit of carrying it with her. Chet had taught her to record her thoughts when they began to work on helping her recover her memory.

The only memories Marine had were those she was creating while starting her new life in New Brook. She opened the journal to its first entry that was written her first night in her new home. As she read, she could picture the scenes as though they were playing before her on a movie screen.

After they left the cruise and flew to Charlotte, Chet and Marine headed for what she now thought of as the best place on Earth to live. She remembered that while driving up

Fancy Gap Mountain, which divided Virginia from North Carolina, she thought that the weather in New Brook was colder.

"Hey, Chet?" Marine leaned forward in her seat.

"Yes?" Chet said as he looked back at Marine using the rear-view mirror.

"Do you remember the first day you drove me into town?"

"Yes. It was a day not much different than this one."

"I remember thinking when we turned down Main Street, just like you're doing now, what a lovely town New Brook looked like to me."

"It's proven to be a good new home for you, hasn't it?" Aunt Betsy turned around and smiled at Marine.

Marine nodded and looked back at her journal. She glanced at the words,

On the ride to New Brook, I decided not to tell Chet about the previous night's events. Drake said I shouldn't. Drake was there right after I fought with Ana-Geliza after she broke into my cabin. I think I killed her.

Marine thought about how quickly she had reacted to Ana-Geliza when she came at her

The Fire of Revenge

with the knife. She turned back a page in her journal and continued reading:

When I hit the floor, my fight-or-flight instincts kicked in, and I reacted like an animal protecting itself with no thought of what I was doing. I rolled to my right side, cocked my left leg, and kicked Ana-Geliza in the crotch with accuracy and force, knocking her back, causing the cabin door to slam shut. It gave me time enough to flip up on my feet. I ran toward the open sliding glass doors in an effort to escape her attack. I saw that the lounge chair was in the middle of the veranda sideways. I turned back in time to see that the she was coming at me with one hand in a low fist. I, somehow, instinctively knew that she was coming at me with a knife. I positioned my body to catch her right arm with my left while my right arm slipped up under her belly as I dipped down using the lounge chair to help me flip her over the railing.

Marine raised her eyes from the journal and looked out the car window. Her thoughts were strong about how she had wanted to kill Ana-Geliza. She prayed she was no longer capable of that kind of anger.

"Chet, the distance between where The Fire Academy is located and Belle's location on Main Street is about how far?

"It is about seven miles. The Fire Academy is actually in the city of Evansham. The rolling farmlands and several horse farms, which are not small by any stretch of the imagination, are slowly being squeezed out by development. I heard last week that the buffer of land we're driving by now, which many citizens of New Brook think of as their town moat, might be the next land sold for development."

"I heard the same thing at my circle meeting last week. Marine, I'm sure you have already picked up on the fact that the people of New Brook have good souls, but they will size a person up real quick when they first meet. It is an Appalachian trait to place a lot of stock in first impressions, as it tells a lot about a person. Any new developers that come here will learn that the ways of mountain folk, especially as you move further into the mountain region, is different from most places."

"These last months, I've learned this little town is an interesting place to live. And, I'm excited about my new job. I just hope I'm able to put my past, whatever it is, behind me."

"Why do you think you will need to do that?"

The Fire of Revenge

"I'm not sure. I just worry that whatever I was before, it may not be something I will want to know."

Chet rubbed his forehead in a slow, determined manner.

"Why do you do that?"

"What?"

"Rub your forehead. You rub it like you're thinking really hard or maybe trying not to get mad. I've seen you do it several times."

"It is a habit I have. It is my way of thinking through tough situations."

"Are you in a tough situation?" she said.

Chet smiled at Marine.

"Seriously, Chet. Is there something wrong?"

"This may seem strange, but I thought if I could help you regain your memory—if I could help you, maybe, just maybe I would help myself. I felt like I needed to do more than what I had been doing. And then, you were there."

"Chet, we still have time. I'm not going anywhere."

As she looked out the window, she wondered if her staying in New Brook was such a good idea. But, more importantly, she realized that she shouldn't say anything about the fight she had with Ana-Geliza. She didn't need to burden Chet and Aunt Betsy with the fact that Ana-Geliza wanted to kill her. Who knows, someone else might want to do the same. She pulled on the seat belt as it felt like it was choking her. She moved it behind her back, leaving it secured across her lap.

"Listen, Marine, do not worry about anything, especially about your past."

"I won't. Far as that goes, I don't know a lot about yours or Aunt Betsy's either. It makes us even.

"There's my *Big Pencil*. I love seeing it. It reminds me of my first day here. Chet told me all about how the New Brook Office Supply has proudly hung the 25-foot realistic yellow, number two Ticonderoga pencil on Main Street for well over fifty years. For most, it is a landmark for coming home. I guess I can say that now, too."

"It is huge, isn't it?" Aunt Betsy said as she got out of the car when Chet had parked in front of Belle's.

"It always looks real to me."

"Me, too."

FIVE

CELEBRATION

Aunt Betsy reached into the trunk and retrieved two cake containers. "I can't wait for you to try my apple streusel cake."

"Oh, no. Aunt Betsy. I don't like apples."

"What?"

Chet and Marine burst into laughter. "She is teasing you, Aunt Betsy."

"Oh you two." Aunt Betsy smiled at Marine, "You have come a long way in spite of not gaining your memory. You were fantastic tonight. You mark my words. You will move up in the ranks before you know it. There isn't a man in the department that can match you and your skill."

"Aunt Betsy, you flatter me. But, there are several, even in my class that are strong and dependable firefighters. I was lucky because I was one of four females. I happened to be the strongest of the four. That was the only reason I was chosen as The Academy Leader."

"As your doctor, I can categorically tell you that you are more valuable than your strength. You know how to think on your feet and you have a quick reaction time. You scored the highest score on the team for running the physical trials. I imagine the Battalion Chief will be asking you to participate in the firefighter games."

"Well. Maybe. We will see."

"We are here," Chet said as he maneuvered the door open. "And, remember, your classmates selected you as Academy Leader, not the instructors."

"Let's go in and get us some good ole dessert," Aunt Betsy said as she walked through the door.

"What's in the other cake carry-all?" Marine said as she walked in behind her.

"My red velvet cake. I wasn't going to let us celebrate this occasion without my prized cake being front and center."

When they walked into Belle's Restaurant, Marine was taken aback. Half the town folk she had met were there. There was a huge banner across the back of the restaurant in big red and yellow letters.

CONGRATULATIONS, MARINE!

Tears started to form, but Aunt Betsy leaned over, "Don't you dare shed a tear."

Stifling a giggle and in a lowered voice, "Leave it to you, Aunt Betsy, to put me in the right spirit of things." Marine walked over to the banner.

Everyone came up and shared their congratulations. There were so many people— some were new acquaintances while others were now considered old friends. David Wayne Foglesong, the newly promoted Fire Captain, who had encouraged her to become a firefighter, was becoming a close friend. He walked up and offered his hand.

Shaking his hand, "It means a lot to me that you are here and still dressed in your full dress uniform. You do look sharp."

"Thank you, ma'am. Your speech was well presented and I might say, your connection to The Bell was very well done."

"Thank you. I guess I should finish greeting everyone. This is so nice and so unexpected."

"You go visit with your peeps. I'll be here ready to celebrate with you when you are finished."

After greeting everyone, she noticed there was a table in the front of the room, set near the center. Aunt Betsy and Chet led her to the center seat.

"You sit here," Chet said.

He and Aunt Betsy sat down on either side of me. Everyone else took a seat.

Wayne stood off to one side and said, "May I have your attention, please?" He waited for the room to quiet down. He smiled at me and continued, "Congratulations, Marine. We have gathered as many of the town's folk that you have met and the members of the firehouse that you will be working with to show you our support."

I winked at Aunt Betsy.

"On behalf of the members of the department, let me be the first to say that we are very proud to welcome you as a member of the New Brook Fire Department Chestnut Mountain Station Three."

The Fire of Revenge

"Thank you. I'm so excited. This is a dream come true for me."

"Tomorrow, you will come to the station and we'll begin to work as a team. Each of us is expecting great things out of you. As the leader of your class, you have demonstrated that you have the muster to show what it takes to be a firefighter. Now the fun work begins. So, without further ado, does everyone have a drink?"

I looked around and realized everyone held a champagne glass.

"Here you go, Marine," Chet said as he handed me a glass, too.

"Before we begin, I would like to make a—"

"Excuse me. I'd like to be the one to make the toast if you don't mind," a man said as he stood up in the back.

"Drake, what are you doing here?"

SIX

....

PRETENSE

Chet walked over to Drake and whispered in his ear. Drake then walked over to the table.

"Hello, Marine. I happened to be in the area for work and decided to drop in here for a bite to eat. I never dreamed I'd see you and a party, too. May I continue?"

She nodded yes.

Drake turned and looked at the guests.

"Will everyone please raise your glasses? Now, for my toast—To Marine, the most talented and sophisticated firefighter on the New Brook Fire Department!" Drake raised his glass and took a sip. Marine drank her glass down in one gulp.

The room clapped and Aunt Betsy stood up. "Ladies and gentlemen. Let's have some dessert."

Chet walked over and took Marine's elbow as he said, "I think you should talk with Drake outside. I will cover for you."

As Marine and Chet walked over to Drake, Aunt Betsy said, "Come on everyone, I'll cut the cake. Marine will be back in a few minutes."

"Come on, Drake. You and Marine can talk in private outside." Chet guided them to the side door.

After Chet had closed the door behind him, Marine turned to Drake and shoved him up against a nearby car.

"What do you mean doing that?"

"Hello, to you, too." Drake smiled and took her into his arms.

"Whoa, Bucko. No, you don't. You can't just waltz in here and act like I've not had any questions. Where have you been? I needed to talk to you. I found your note in the Jeep that you wouldn't be at graduation. Yet, you conveniently show up at the party. What gives?"

"Okay. Let's talk."

The Fire of Revenge

"You don't get it, do you? I want to shoot you where you stand." Drake took a step back. "Don't worry. I don't have a gun on me this minute. But, you are going to explain it all to me. Right now. Right this minute."

"Your memory. Has it come back?"

"No. But I'm having flashes."

"Marine, listen to me. It is way too complicated to explain it here. I guess I should have warned you I was in town. When I got into town, I was so happy to hear about your graduation and the party they were giving you. I don't know. My need to talk with you got the better of my good judgment. Since I'm here, can we make plans to meet? I will answer your questions. I promise."

Staring into his eyes; he blinked.

"Don't go promising something you have no intention of delivering." Marine turned and started to walk back into Belle's. Drake grabbed her arm. "Let go, or I'll break it."

"Listen, Marine. Please give me a chance. Meet me at The Edith Hotel tonight. I'm staying there. I'm in Room Three Forty-Two. Meet me at eight o'clock. What do you say?"

She looked at him again. She saw desire in his eyes. She imagined him kissing her, loving her, ravishing her. The longing in her own heart made her want him. His touch would make it all real.

"Okay. I'll meet you. I don't think we should meet in your room. We'll meet in the lobby."

He smiled. "Good. But I think we should meet in the room. What I have to share with you, you should hear in private. May I come back in with you to celebrate?"

"No. I think it's best that you go. I have enough to do. I have to come up with an explanation of who you are and what is going on between us. Far as that goes, I expect you to explain just what is going on between us, tonight. Got it?"

"Yes, ma'am. I got it. I'll see you then."

* * * * *

Marine walked back into Belle's and Chet met her as she made her way across the dining room.

"What did Drake say?"

"Nothing much. I'm going to meet him later at The Edith. He evidently has been staying there for some time. Did you know he was in town?"

The Fire of Revenge

"I saw a man the other day who I thought looked like him, but I never was able to get a close enough look. I chose not to say anything to you. Did he say any more?"

"No. He didn't. Let me see if I can smooth this over, especially with Wayne. He's headed this way."

"Hello!" Wayne said as he handed Marine a slice of cake and another glass of champagne. "Want to sit?"

"Thanks." Marine took what he offered as she motioned to some seats at a nearby table. "I guess you're wondering what that was all about."

Wayne nodded his head. "You can tell me what you think I need to know. I'm cool with whatever is going on. You seem tense."

"Drake Bianchi was the photographer on the cruise where I met Dr. Chet. He helped me when I was attacked. We're friends."

"Attacked?"

"Yes. A woman broke into my cabin the last night we were on the ship and fought with me. She acted like she was trying to kill me. Drake managed to get into my room and help me. She was my cabin steward. Drake told me later that he had no idea what she was up to. I have no idea why she was trying to hurt me. Anyway, when I came here with Chet, I began to leave all that behind me. I was surprised to see Drake tonight."

"I can imagine. Did Chet know this man was in town?"

"I don't think so. He seemed as surprised as I was."

Marine looked into Wayne's eyes as he took her hand. She thought about telling all she knew, but then realized she couldn't. What more was there really to tell? She had revealed what little she knew. Chet didn't even know about her suspicions of who she thought she was. She couldn't tell Wayne when he didn't even know about her memory loss.

"And, one more thing, Chet doesn't know about the fight on the ship."

"He doesn't?"

"No."

Wayne looked at Marine.

"Can I explain this all to you later?"

"Sure." Wayne moved his chair back. "Enough of this for now. Let's go visit with your fans. Everyone wants to congratulate you. You'll be working with some really good guys; some are here tonight. And, Battalion Chief

Whisman wants to formally present you to the shift tomorrow. I have a feeling you're going to do well."

Marine smiled and tried to forget about Drake. Becoming a firefighter was a new beginning for her. The past, whatever it was, will not interfere with her future.

SEVEN

....

REVELATION 101

The knock at the door came an hour too early, Drake thought as he got up off the plush bed in his room. He wondered who it could be.

The rooms in The Edith were designed in an antebellum-style and were lavishly decorated. The hotel had been a travel destination for years. People from all over made travel plans to stop in New Brook. Some came to see the colorful fall leaves, others to explore the beauty of the area by hiking and mountain bike riding or to enjoy motorcycle rides on the nearby Blue Ridge Parkway. During December, the hotel was a luxurious place to enjoy the season and the ambiance of the surrounding mountain views and tranquil setting.

"You must have the wrong room," Drake said as he opened the door expecting a guest to be trying to find his or her way around.

"No, I think I have the right one," Chet said as he walked in. "May I come in?"

"Why are you here?"

"Because, Marine is confused enough without you grandstanding. What was that all about this evening?"

"I was happy to see how well she was doing. I'm sorry if I was out of line by showing up like I did."

"You could ruin everything. I've worked so hard to help her gain her memory. A shock like that could have been dangerous. What did you talk about?"

"Nothing, really. I told her we should meet tonight. I plan on telling her everything then."

"Why? What good does it do? She is making great progress. You do not need to reveal all that horrid mess, do you?"

"Look, when we were on the ship, I agreed with you that we should wait. I came to you because of the danger she was in. I shared I was with MI6 and told you we had her under surveillance. All that has now changed."

"Why? What has happened?"

"TRANS has folded. Due to the intelligence leaks that revealed how governments worked with companies like TRANS, many countries like the States are no longer funding such operations. The heads of these companies are fleeing to avoid prosecution. Even MI6 is having a reduction in connections with these types. I still have my job, but there are many within TRANS that are now freelance assassins and rogue dealers waiting for a job to come their way."

"Okay. That is good for Marine. She does not have to worry about TRANS or even need to know about them."

"Well, no. Not exactly."

"Why? Why not?"

"Ana-Geliza is in town. She's probably here gunning for Marine. We have to tell Marine so she can protect herself. Ana-Geliza is cunning. She was Marine's second for a reason."

"Marine's second? What does that mean? You never told me that before."

"At the time, I thought it best not to reveal that part. Ana-Geliza was the understudy to Marine. She was a good agent in her own right."

"A good agent?"

"I mean she was good at what she did. But, as Marine's second, she was privy to a lot of details about Marine. The complicated part was that Marine did not know that Ana-Geliza was her second before she lost her memory. And, I had no idea that Ana-Geliza was planning to go rogue. She made that clear when she attacked Marine the last night on the ship."

"What?"

"Marine didn't tell you?" Chet shook his head. "As Marine's steward on the ship, she had access to a lot of information on her. Evidently, Ana-Geliza blames Marine for her personal failure in life and she has chosen to do Marine in. The information from MI6 is that Ana-Geliza will stop at nothing to finish her final target, which is Marine."

"Drake, we cannot tell her this without preparing her. She could have a significant reaction. She is starting to believe in her future and in herself. I have managed to help her remember some things as being dreams. I do not think she could handle learning she was a covert agent involved in assassinations and espionage without laying some proper groundwork. You cannot just blurt it out."

The Fire of Revenge

"Doc, I get your concern. But, Marine was a strong woman before. She is still a strong woman now. If we don't warn her about the danger, she could fall into a major trap—and this time, I may not be there to help her."

"Okay. I see your point. But can you maybe do this over a few days, or even a week? Give me time to talk with her and guide her through this new information."

"I don't know when Ana-Geliza will strike and I don't know how much danger everyone is in that associated with Marine. Do you understand? Ana-Geliza doesn't mind having collateral damage. Her goal is to take out Marine. That's all she is focused on at this moment."

"Do you have any idea where she is now?"

"The last we heard, she was headed in this direction. That was a week ago. For all I know, she is in town hiding, like a mulga dragon—remaining motionless and unobserved—allowing her to ambush Marine when ready."

EIGHT

....

A MOMENT IN TIME

Walking over to the elevator of The Edith was not what Marine thought she would be doing. She wished Drake had been willing to meet in the lobby. Why did he have to show up now, of all days? She pressed the button to go up. His room was on the third floor. While waiting for the elevator to arrive, an elderly couple ambled up beside her.

"George, I told you we never stayed here before," The petite woman in stature, who looked to be eighty-eight or ninety years old said with a voice that crackled. "I'm not going to argue. We were in a different city."

The elderly gentleman looked over at Marine and smiled. "She doesn't even know where we are."

As suddenly as the elevator doors opened, the woman hit her husband with her purse. "I might be old, but I'm not deaf. I do so know where we are. We're in this blasted hotel in a town that isn't right. Now, get on this blasted elevator so we can go to the wrong room."

Marine stifled a giggle. The old couple had distracted her. She chastised herself. Keep your wits. You don't need your guard down, now.

As she stepped off the elevator into the hallway, she had a flashback to when she and Drake were walking toward her cruise cabin. He was leading the way, holding her hand. She felt light headed and longed for his touch. "Gees, Marine. Get a grip," she chided herself aloud as she reached the door of room Three Forty-Two. Turning and walking away is not an option. She knocked.

"Hello," Drake said as he swung the door wide open. "Come on in."

"You sound like a spider asking a fly to come into your web."

"Funny, you should think of me as a spider. Aren't Black Widows female?"

"The ones who kill?"

"Yes."

"I guess so. Are you trying to tell me something?"

"Can we at least get in the room and have a polite conversation before we dig into the ugliness of our lives?"

Marine turned and faced him. "Look, you're the one that insisted on this meeting. I would just as soon never lay eyes on you again."

Drake took one step closer and pulled Marine into his arms. She tried to resist, but his scent and his strength were more powerful than her distaste for him. She longed for him to hold her, to caress her, to take her.

"Oh, Drake." It had been too long since she was last in a man's arms.

"Marine," he kissed her passionately. Then, he slowly pushed her back away from his face. "We've got to stop this. We must talk." He walked over to the bar. "Would you like a drink?"

"Wait a minute. We haven't seen each other in months. Well, at least, I haven't seen you. Just now, we connected as though we've always been together. And now, you want to stop and have a drink? What gives? Why are you here?"

"I have to share some things with you that I believe you need to know. It is about your past. Will you sit and let me explain?"

Marine stood there and began to tap her foot. Her anger mounted. "Does Chet know about this?"

"What makes you ask?"

"He seemed strange earlier. It was as though he knew you were going to talk to me about my past. What does Chet know?"

"Marine, please sit down."

"Why is it when people are going to tell you awful info, they always want you to sit?"

"Maybe they don't want you to bolt."

"Bolt? Bolt! How about I shoot you instead?"

"Do you even own a gun?"

"No. Oh hell. What am I doing? Drake, I'm so confused. And, now I'm scared." She walked over to him. "I guess I'll take a drink after all. Give me a scotch. Put a drop of water in it. No ice."

"That's funny. I was ready to fix you a Manhattan. I had the bar downstairs stock mine with all the ingredients. Scotch it is."

Marine walked over to the window and looked out. The room was situated over the backside of the hotel with a view of Downtown

The Fire of Revenge

New Brook. In the distance, the lights from the shopping center showed brightly. Off to the right was a dark area, which was where the town butted up against the Blue Ridge Parkway. She turned and waited for Drake to continue.

"Okay. Here you go," Drake handed Marine her drink. "I fixed myself one, too. Let's sit here." He pointed to the couch. Marine chose the chair next to the window. Looking out gave her the feeling she could escape.

"Shall we begin?" She took a sip.

"Do you remember Ana-Geliza?" Marine nodded she did. "Well, she is in town."

Marine took another sip. "Okay. That means when I thought I caught a glimpse of her last night, I didn't imagine it."

"You saw her last night?"

"Yes. And, last week I thought I saw you, too. Did I?"

"I don't think so."

Marine laughed. "What do you mean 'you don't think so'? Either you do or you don't. Did you see me when I saw you?"

"No. I didn't see you because I didn't arrive here this time until yesterday."

"This time?"

"As you know, I followed you and Chet here when you first arrived. I've been back here a couple of times since. Then, about a month ago, I had to return to work to gather more information. I was recently given clearance to continue with this surveillance. I jumped on the first flight from London and arrived in New Brook yesterday afternoon."

"Wow. London. Really? I had no idea a photographer had so many jobs around the globe. So, what kind of photo gigs do you really do?"

"Marine. You have to listen and you have to understand. I wanted to tell you all of this, months ago."

"Months ago? I've only known you a little more than eight months, haven't I?"

"Well, not exactly. In your lost memory, you would know we've known each other a lot longer."

"Every time I think I am starting to understand who I was, I find there is someone holding out. Just spit it out. Who was I?"

"I can't."

"Why not?"

"Because, I've been advised to take it slow. I'm going to honor those wishes and let you know that I'm here to protect you and to be there when you need me."

"Why do you need to protect me?"

"I work for an organization that wants to protect you because of things you may not remember."

"Drake, all I seem to remember about you is holding me; every time I touch you, I flashback to you caressing me and us having passionate sex. Have I dreamed that or was it real? And, what is so dangerous about it if it was?"

Drake laughed. He got up and walked over to the bar, "Would you like a refill?"

"No. I want you to get to the point. Who are you?"

"Drake Bianchi." Drake handed Marine a white, linen card. It read 'Drake Bianchi, Special Intelligence, London, England.'

"You really are from London?" Drake nodded. "I thought you were pulling my leg. So, what does this all have to do with me and my past?"

"Without going into a lot of details, let me try to give you some background. Ana-Geliza was your cabin steward. She also worked for a company, TRANS, which stands for Terminate, Reeducate, Assassinate, Neutralize, and

Sabotage. The company, Transcontinental Solutions, was an international company that conducted espionage and other related jobs to help countries and those in power to shape the events of the world that would help them prosper. As an agent of TRANS, she was assigned the task of completing assassination jobs if her immediate supervisor failed at his or her job. Ana-Geliza was in her final stages of training. When you met her on the cruise, she was there to finish her last assignment. She would have been promoted to agent status. But, you interrupted that when you fell and lost your memory."

"Me? How in the world would that—" Marine suddenly had a memory flash of when she first met Ana-Geliza on the ship and how she had had a feeling of concern about her. At the time, Marine didn't think much about it. But now, hearing Drake's story, she began to wonder just who she was. "Are you telling me I was involved with these people?"

"No. I'm not telling you that. I'm merely saying that Ana-Geliza blames you for her not making the grade. The bad part is that TRANS has since folded due to security leaks. The governments that worked with companies like

The Fire of Revenge

TRANS have shut down their operations. Ana-Geliza is without a job, but she still has her skill and knowledge of how to kill. She is a rogue agent who is looking for you. I'm here to protect you and to help you."

Marine sat there taking in all of what Drake had said, but she had trouble believing him. Puzzled as to what she should do next, she stood up. Walking over to the bar where Drake stood, she placed her drink down, and then walked to the door.

She turned to him and said as sternly as she could muster, "You realize that you sound incredibly scary. Worse, you sound crazy. I'm leaving now. You are not to come anywhere near me. Do you hear me?"

As Marine reached for the doorknob, Drake moved toward her and grabbed her shoulders to stop her.

Marine twisted away from him and said, "Leave me alone."

Drake dropped his hands; she turned and walked out the door.

NINE

....

AWAKENING

Chet opened the door to Trout House Falls, Aunt Betsy's home, to find Marine standing on the porch before him rubbing her shoulder.

"What happened?"

"I'll explain. Let's get inside. I need a drink."

Chet led Marine to the sofa in the den. "Tell me, what did Drake say?"

* * * * *

The next morning, Marine got up and made her way downstairs to the kitchen. Aunt Betsy was cooking one of Marine's favorite breakfasts—country sausage, waffles, and warmed maple syrup with fresh, brewed coffee.

"Ah, this smells heavenly. Can you imagine

if they made a perfume that smelled like this?"

"Good morning to you, too, and they do. Actually, it is a candle perfumed with the morning breakfast smell. I thought since it was a cold, winter morning, we would have a hearty meal to help us get going."

Marine walked over to the coffee pot, poured a mug full, and began to add sugar and cream. "Well, you chose a good morning to do it. I'm supposed to be down at the station about nine thirty to meet with the Battalion Chief and Captain Wayne. After last night's meeting with Drake, I'm ready to get on with my life and leave all those other people out of it."

Marine moved to the bay window and looked out at the view. The driveway wound up along a small hill. It was bound by a row of oak trees on both sides. At the end of the road sat Aunt Betsy's two-story 1870 Victorian brick home at the crest of a gentle slope. It had an immaculate front yard landscaped to perfection and a view of New Brook that matched.

Aunt Betsy broke the silence. "Chet said you had a hard time of it with Drake. How are you?"

"I'll be fine. I sure wanted to break Drake's head. The nerve of that guy." Marine walked over to the kitchen table and sat down.

The Fire of Revenge

Chet walked in, "Good morning you two. How are you feeling?"

"I'm doing well, Chet. Thank you," Aunt Betsy grinned; she set a plate down in front of Marine.

"Funny." Chet gave Aunt Betsy a kiss on the cheek. "Marine, how are *you* doing?"

"I'm fine, too, Chet. How are you?"

"Good. I would like to plan to talk with you this morning before you leave for the station. Can we do that?"

"I don't know. It's like I tried to explain to you last night. I don't want to hear what Drake has to say. None of it makes sense and I really don't want to have to try to figure it all out. I have a feeling I'm not going to like whatever he has to say."

"Marine, you probably won't. But, it might mean your safety."

"How could someone as small and out of control as Ana-Geliza possibly hurt me? She's already tried once. She failed. I'm not afraid of her or anybody else as far as that goes. I don't need anyone's help, especially Drake's."

"You may not. But, it does not hurt to have him close by. You never know. As Drake told you, Ana-Geliza has been working on ways to cause you pain for a while now."

"Drake tried to tell me that. How am I supposed to act on something like that? How am I supposed to be prepared? Even Drake has no idea how she will attack next. Isn't it better to live life and react when something happens rather than to always be scared and on guard? I don't want to live that way."

"May I interject something?" Aunt Betsy said as she placed Chet's plate in front of him.

"Sure," Marine said. She wiped the remaining syrup on her plate with her last bite of waffle.

"Why don't you go to the police and tell them what you know?"

"Yeah, why don't we do that?" She looked at Chet.

"You cannot," Chet said, as he placed a third pat of butter on his waffle. "Drake said the local police would not understand the workings of an agent like Ana-Geliza. Drake told me that he is the only one that can help Marine until she gets her memory back. He said that only trained agents, like him, would know how to react to Ana-Geliza and her attacks."

"That's another thing. Why is it always 'Drake said'? Furthermore, as Drake has told

The Fire of Revenge

you, why is it the case that I will be able to help myself when my memory returns, but I can't now? Does that mean I'm a trained agent, too? Was I an assassin?"

"You do not need to dwell on that. You need to rely on Drake. He can help you and he is aware of how Ana-Geliza works. You have put your trust in me to help you regain your memory. Why do you resist trusting me to guide you now?"

"Yes, I do trust your help with my memory. What you're doing is working. I've been having flashbacks and I'm starting to remember portions of my past."

"You are remembering more than what you have been sharing with me?"

Chet put his fork down and Aunt Betsy sat down in a chair at the table.

"Yes. Last night, after my fight with Drake, I remembered that I worked in a tall office building, but I'm not sure where it was located. I don't remember any details other than I know I met Drake there."

"How do you know you met Drake there?" Chet said as he leaned closer to Marine.

"I'm not sure. I know that I did, though. And, in a funny way, I think I remember seeing

Ana-Geliza there, but her hair was a different color and she wore glasses." Marine looked down at her plate and placed her head in her hands. "I don't know." She looked up and said, "It's all jumbled. Yet, I feel it's all coming together. I know I'm close."

"Speaking of close, it is close to the time for you to leave." Aunt Betsy got up, walked over to the counter, and then set a brown paper bag on the table. "I packed you a lite lunch—an apple, a cup of mixed nuts with yogurt covered raisins, and a bottle of green tea. You'll need a healthy snack after you go through some of your indoctrination today."

Marine got up out of her chair, took her dishes to the sink, and bent down to give Aunt Betsy a kiss on the cheek.

"Thanks. You're the bestest aunt any girl could have."

"That's sweet. But, I'd like for you to think of me as more than an aunt."

Marine walked to the doorway, and then turned back, "Chet, please don't give up on me. I am doing the best I can. Right now, I want to go start my new life. My past doesn't need to interfere with that right now."

TEN

OH, MY CAPTAIN

Aunt Betsy's Jeep started right up in spite of the cold air. Marine drove directly to the New Brook Chestnut Mountain Fire Station Three where Wayne served as Captain. She had been told to meet him at nine thirty. With five minutes to spare, after parking in the lot, she gathered her belongings and locked up the Jeep. She smiled to herself.

Marine turned to walk into the firehouse. A strange feeling rippled down her spine. She rubbed her eyes.

For a moment, she thought she was looking at a skyscraper in a city near the water. She looked up. The sky was bright and sunny. A stark contrast to how it seemed just moments ago—a typical dreary, winter day with a light, cold breeze blowing her hair.

"Hey! Are you okay?"

Marine heard someone calling, but she felt as though she wasn't in the same place. Then, she felt a hand on her shoulder.

"I've been calling your name. Are you okay?"

Marine turned and looked into Wayne's eyes. "Yes. Yes, I'm fine. I think I was blinded by the sun's rays all of a sudden."

"What sun?"

She looked up only to see a dark overcast sky. "Oh, I guess I was thinking of something else. Well, I'm here as instructed, sir."

"Congratulations on being appointed to Station Three – Chestnut Mountain."

"Thank you, sir. I look forward to learning all I can."

* * * * *

"First, I need to begin to help you understand about our time sheets and how scheduling works. And, let me say in the beginning, it is complicated. It takes lots of people several time periods before they begin to get the hang of it. Have you ever worked under the Federal Fair Labor Standards Act?"

The Fire of Revenge

"I don't think so."

"Don't be concerned if you don't understand it at first. The main thing you need to remember is that your work time is considered on an individual basis. You shouldn't think of it as how everyone works. You are allowed to work one hundred and sixty hours within a twenty-eight day time-period. After that, you will have time off. But, that time off can be cut short with the need to fill in if someone is sick or on vacation."

"You mean I may have to work overtime?"

"Yes. This means you can elect to take the overtime as pay at time and one-half or you can have the hours off during the next pay period. Do you understand me so far?"

"I think so."

"Most people relate to office jobs and working in industry for forty hour weeks. Our time is hard to understand. It will take you a few months, but you'll catch on."

"Okay. I'll let you know if I have questions. I'm so excited about this job. I don't think I'll have an issue."

"Maybe. So, let me show you around now."

Wayne gave Marine a tour of the building, showing her the bunkroom, the kitchen, and, of course, the trucks. They spent about two hours talking about the equipment and tools and how they were different from what she had been introduced to at The Academy.

"You'll find that—" Wayne turned.

"Hello." Marine read his nametag. He was one of the battalion chiefs that she briefly met at graduation. "Chief Whisman. It's nice to meet you."

"Hello, Chief," Wayne said. "Since you had to leave early, you didn't get to formally meet Marine at graduation. I'd like to introduce to you our newest recruit, Firefighter Marine Letsco. Marine, Battalion Chief Whisman."

Chief Whisman extended his hand; Marine shook it. He had a strong grip.

"Glad to have you aboard. I'm sorry we didn't get time to speak at graduation. You gave a very nice speech." Marine nodded. "Wayne is showing you the ropes, yes?"

"Yes, sir. He is indeed. I'm not sure I'll remember all he's shown me, but I'll study hard."

The Chief patted Marine on the back. "No need to worry about what you remember right now. You're on probation until you complete your first six weeks. So enjoy your new surroundings and learn how to function with firehouse life. Wayne, has she been issued her gear yet?"

"No, sir. We are doing that next."

"I'll be around the house until I must go up on the hill for a staff meeting. You go about what you're doing. Letsco, I like that name. You will fit in well around here."

As Chief Whisman turned to go, Wayne mentioned that they would be meeting the rest of her shift at Belle's for lunch.

"You have been assigned to work with C Shift, due to a vacancy. There are nine firefighters on the shift including you and me. Right now, most of them are out doing company inspections." He looked at his watch. "We have about an hour before we'll need to leave to meet them. Let's go assign your locker." Wayne stopped speaking and started to laugh.

Marine looked at him, "What's so funny?"

They started to walk to the locker room. "Let's go, Letsco." He laughed again. "Don't you get it?"

"Yeah, I get it. I put up with that all the time at TRANS."

Marine froze in her steps.

"Letsco, you okay?"

"Yeah. I am." Marine shook off her sudden feelings of anger and fear. "What were you saying?"

"I said we'll provide you with firehouse turnout gear—you know, the stuff you wear to fight a fire."

"Funny."

"You're listening now." He smiled. "The fire gear you used at The Academy you can store at home and use if you need to report while you're off duty. You'll need to go get fitted for your dress uniform. It takes about two weeks before it will be ready. Do you have any questions?"

"No, sir. Not yet."

They walked over to the lockers that hung on the wall next to the office.

"Good. Now, here is your locker for your turnout gear. We'll also assign you a personal locker that is located in the bunkroom. Here is your lock with the combination. Try not to lose the combo if you can help it. We do have a master list, so make sure what you place in here you don't mind it being searched if need be. Any questions?"

Marine smiled at him, as he seemed so formal. "No, sir."

The Fire of Revenge

He smiled back.

"Let's go get your turnout gear. We'll be going to Supply, which is located at Station One. Why don't you get your coat? We'll ride over there together, and then go to Belle's."

* * * * *

After going through the process to fit Marine for her turnout gear and get her uniforms sized properly, Wayne made sure the seamstress spelled her last name correctly. Then, he turned to Marine.

"Well, now, you are almost official. We're about ready to go have a special lunch at Belle's. It will give you a chance to meet the rest of the shift before we have to get down to work."

"How many did you say I'd be working with?"

"There are seven others. A lieutenant and two sergeants and the rest are firefighters, like you. Though, you are a Probie, so to speak. You'll learn they each have a nickname. I'll let you figure out who's who."

"The new guy always gets the bum's rush, I take it."

"I haven't heard that saying in a long time." Wayne smiled as he opened the door for her. "Here we are. I'll introduce you. You follow my lead."

They walked into Belle's and were immediately surrounded by some of the locals that Marine had seen the night before. After making their general greetings and thanking Belle again for the graduation party, they sat down with the rest of the shift. A couple of tables had been pulled together for them all to fit.

"Well, guys, let me introduce you to our new Probie. Actually, some of you have met her, but we're going to do this formal. Now, you need to know, this Probie isn't all that much a girl. She actually has some skill. We believe she will be as strong as anyone will when it comes to being a firefighter. She was named the Fire Academy Leader, after all. This, gentlemen, is Probie Marine Letsco."

Marine watched the faces of the men as Wayne introduced her. She felt funny hearing him talk about her while she sat there. Yet, she had a suspicion she might be as good as any of them. Their faces were a mixed bag of interest and smirks as Wayne spoke. She knew it would

The Fire of Revenge

be a tough gang to connect with, but she was determined to be one of the guys.

"Hello, Probie. I'm Sergeant George Fisher. Wayne told me I'd be your FTO."

"Glad to meet you, George." She looked questioningly at Wayne.

"You can call me Fish and before you finish your tenure as a Probie, we'll give you a proper nickname, too. I saw you look at Wayne when I said 'FTO.' It stands for Field Training Officer. It is my duty to save your butt when we go into fires. Just because you're fresh out of The Academy, doesn't mean you won't need help or support when we're working an active fire; you can't be on the fire ground without me by your side. Capiche?" Marine nodded to him. "Until you receive your helmet and coat with your name all over it, you'll be wearing our backup turn-out gear. So get ready, Probie. When the fire call comes in, you're hitting the ground."

"If I can wear the backup turnout gear, why does my name have to be all over everything?"

"That way we can find you when you fall on your face."

The group busted out laughing.

"Easy, guys." Wayne stepped forward. "At least let her meet everyone before you begin ragging on her. Now, each of you, introduce yourself. We'll skip Fish since he's already done that."

The group went around the table introducing themselves. After Fish, there were four firefighters of different ranks – Gary "Crab" Potts, Greg "Cotton Top" Brooks, Dennis "Willie" Ray, Charlie "Doc" White. Ron James, the nearest to me, stood up and shook my hand.

"Hello, Marine. I'm Ron James, your Lieutenant. My nickname is LT. Let's just say, that if Fish doesn't kick your butt, I will most assuredly."

"Glad to meet you, I think." Marine smiled back.

"I guess I'm last. I'm Roy Rogers, the other Sergeant of the shift. You won't get any trouble out of me as long as you don't cause me to get burned."

Marine went to shake Roy's hand but found she was laughing instead.

"Are you serious?"

"Look Probie, you can't join in that game yet. Yes, my name really is Roy Rogers, which means my nickname is?"

The Fire of Revenge

"Surely, it's not Dale?" Everyone laughed as he grabbed her into a bear hug.

She reacted by almost kicking him in the groin. She saw Wayne move. He blocked her knee. The reaction to hit Roy in the groin was split second.

"Oh, I'm sorry. My foot went out from under me," She said to Roy as she broke away.

"No problem, Sweetie. Nah, I don't have a nickname. Some people call me Dale for a joke. But, I go by Roy." His grin was large, his teeth sparkled, and Marine noticed he wore his uniform with perfect creases. Roy returned to his seat. He was dapper.

"Let's all get down to ordering—we need to get back to our jobs, and I have some assignments for Marine and Fish."

Belle walked up and said, "Okay. I have your orders placed. Wayne and Marine, I put in your usual. Now, does anyone want anything other than tea?"

"I'd like some milk if you don't mind, Belle," Marine said as she returned to her seat.

"Sure thing, Sweetie. Your food should be up shortly."

The guys began talking about different things they were encountering while making their inspections. Marine was intrigued by the manner in which the guys interacted with each other. It was clear that Roy was the jokester and Fish was the one that kept everyone in order. Wayne and LT sat back and observed everyone, including Marine. She kept catching Wayne staring.

"Captain?"

"Yes, Letsco."

"I was wondering. You said you'd have some assignments for me. What will they be?"

Belle walked up carrying some of the order. She began to place different dishes down in front of each of the men. Fish got a vegetable platter with soup while Roy got a cheese sandwich with veggie soup. Some of the guys had hamburgers while others had the special of the day, which was spaghetti with garlic toast.

"Captain, what did you and Letsco get?" Roy reached for the catsup. "I love the French fries here."

"Never you mind. You eat your food. We'll get ours soon enough."

Belle came around and filled each of the glasses with either tea or ice water. "I'll bring you a fresh milk, Marine when I bring yours and Wayne's order."

The Fire of Revenge

"Thanks, Belle."

"Well, isn't that sweet," Crab, who sat at the end of the table, said to Fish.

"Don't be a fool," She could hear Fish reply. "The Captain will have your head."

"I ain't scared of the Captain," Crab replied.

"You should be," Wayne said as he had gotten up and walked behind Crab and hit the back of his head.

"Oh, you just got Gibbed!" Fish said with a laugh.

"What is 'Gibbed'?" Marine asked LT.

"Do you watch the TV show, NCIS?" Marine shook her head no. "The lead NCIS agent played by Mark Harmon is named Agent Gibbs. Whenever one of his agents does something foolish or Gibbs wants to remind his agents who is in charge, he'll smack the back of their heads. It is referred to as a *Gibb*."

"Guess that is a show I should watch."

"You would be wise to do so," LT said as he winked at her.

Belle brought out the BLT with egg sandwiches that were made with well-toasted whole wheat and had a pile of curly fries. Marine had fallen in love with that sandwich the first time she ate breakfast at Belle's.

Belle set a platter in front of her; Marine looked at LT and Fish. "I had no idea that it was also Wayne's favorite sandwich until he ordered it, too. It has become a standing joke in Belle's that Wayne and I are the only ones to get egg on our sandwich after eleven in the morning."

Marine noticed Fish smacking Roy on the back of the head.

Everyone must have been hungry, as each ate quietly. When lunch was over, they went their separate ways except for Wayne and Marine. They walked out to his vehicle together; he touched Marine's hand.

"Wait a minute, Marine." Marine turned to him. His face looked grave. "Marine, I'm speaking to you now as a friend. We have to stop being friendly while we're at work. You have to treat me as your Captain. Don't call me Wayne unless you put Captain in front of it. I can't have insubordination in my ranks."

Marine was stunned. "Wayne, you're the one that said we'd go to Belle's. You didn't stop Belle from ordering our sandwich. You introduced me as some female 'Rocky.' And now, I'm the one who is displaying insubordination." She bit her lip, deciding not to speak. The bite had brought blood.

"Letsco, we'll head to the station and I'll put you on your first assignment."

Marine and Wayne got into the car. As he backed out of the parking spot, he said, "Sorry about that. I saw Ron and a couple of the other guys walking toward us. I didn't want them to get the wrong idea."

"No, I don't think you would."

"I hear a tone in your voice."

"A tone? Really. I did not mean to have sounded like I have a tone, Captain."

"Come on. We're in the car now. You don't have to be so formal."

"No, sir. I do. If I let down my guard too much, I'll cause you harm, Captain. We can't have that now, can we?"

Wayne pulled the car over to the side of the road and stopped. He turned to Marine and took her hand. "Listen to me. I didn't mean to say anything that hurt you."

Marine took her hand out of his. "You did. It is done. Let's leave it at that. I won't do anything that will cause insubordination. You don't have to worry about that, sir."

Wayne looked straight ahead as Marine wished she could get out of the vehicle and walk away. "This will be tough on us. It will be hard. But, we can do it. Besides, I may be your Captain, but I'd like for us to remain friends. Who knows what the future holds for us." Wayne stuck out his hand to Marine.

Marine shook his hand.

"Now that we have that settled, we'll be Captain and Probie."

"Right."

ELEVEN

....

TORN

After the initial couple of days, Marine's work fell into a routine. It was moments of joy mixed with frustration and high anxiety. She continued to learn about the operations of the firehouse, as well as the policies and procedures of the overall fire department. She also was learning how her life would be affected by having Wayne as her boss and Drake always checking in.

"Do you receive your full turnout gear tomorrow?" Aunt Betsy asked as Marine took the bowl of mashed potatoes and placed them on the dining room table.

"Yes. I will finally have everything. I'm supposed to also get my dress uniforms. At least, now, when I go to a fire, they'll be able to find me with my name on my backside."

Aunt Betsy laughed, "What do you mean?"

Marine demonstrated how the turnout coat stopped in the middle of her thighs. Then, when she would bend over, her name would be along the bottom of the tail of her coat; it would sit prominently on her hips. She and Aunt Betsy laughed aloud at the sight she described while she bent over.

"Somebody must have gotten good news," Chet said as he walked into the dining room. "The smell wafting into the den called me before you had a chance, Aunt Betsy. I am hungry. But, the laughter is contagious."

"Good. Marine and I have been working like slaves for you. It's about time you came in here to enjoy this fine meal. And, we had a good laugh, too."

"Are you going to share what was so funny?"

"You had to have been here," Marine said as she placed another bowl on the table.

"You can explain it again."

"Nope. It won't be as funny," Aunt Betsy threw her arms up in the air and went back to the kitchen.

"I heard you say that you get all your gear tomorrow. Well done, Marine."

The Fire of Revenge

"Thanks, Chet. I'm thrilled, too. I'm looking forward to seeing how it all fits."

Aunt Betsy set down the main dish, a pork loin that was still sizzling from its recent stay in the oven. "Well, I think it's all out and ready. You both washed up?"

"Yes, ma'am. I'm starving." Marine said as she positioned herself in her chair. Dishes moved back and forth, as they each filled their own plates.

"Have you already been with the department two weeks?" Chet asked as he placed a second slice of homemade bread on his plate and reached for the butter.

"Yes. I have a feeling that time will continue to seem like it is flying by. I mean I feel like I just started as a firefighter. I think that once I get to fight a fire, I'll be so involved that I won't notice time. Captain said the other day he hadn't remembered such a dry spell for several years."

"Dry spell?" Aunt Betsy reached for the mashed potatoes. "Really? I'd think you'd be pleased."

"Well, we are, Aunt Betsy. It is just that we are used to having a call or two a day. Many times the calls have been nothing—or if there *is* a fire, it seems like the fire puts itself out before the pumper arrives. But, even so, we haven't been on a major fire call since I started. Captain Wayne says that I've caused the dry spell."

Chet chuckled, "He might be right. Have you talked with Drake lately?"

"Chet, do we have to talk about him now?"

"I was hoping to hear that you are cooperating with Drake and allowing him to stay near you."

"It's been a little hard, since most days I've been at the firehouse. But, starting tomorrow, I move to the second shift. Instead of days, I'll work with C Shift from eight to eight. It should make things easier."

"Lordy be. Twelve-hour shifts. Those used to kill me."

"When did you work twelve-hour shifts, Aunt Betsy?"

"When I was a young girl. I worked at the local sugar factory on the other side of the city. Of course, back then it was in the county. The city line stopped a good eight miles back."

"There was a sugar factory here?" Marine asked as she reached for another roll. "I had no idea they grew sugar in this area. What did you do there?"

"Oh, the factory wasn't here. I was in Montana. It was during World War II. They moved the interred Japanese inland to work on the beet farms; most of the farmers had no idea how to raise beets for sugar so they used the Japanese because they were familiar with sugar beet production. My grandpa was one of those farmers that needed help. I worked alongside several very nice Japanese. It's where I met my first love." Aunt Betsy said as she winked at Chet.

"Your first love? Tell me more, and why did you wink?"

"You saw that, did you? I winked because most people think since I'm an old woman without any children that I'm a spinster. Most people are wrong." Aunt Betsy smiled and looked off in the distance.

"Aunt Betsy, you can tell Marine more about your story later. Tell me, Marine, how will working this new shift allow Drake to be with you more?"

"It just seems like it will be easier. He'll be able to talk with me and we can check out places he thinks Ana-Geliza might be hiding.

When I'm at the firehouse in the evening, he shouldn't have to worry about me too much as I'll be with eight other guys that can help protect me."

"Did Drake tell you that?"

"No. I decided it would work well for him. Why?"

"Marine, Drake has been over at this house every day, pacing the floor. He's worried sick about you and wants you to let him help you more," Aunt Betsy said as she retrieved another slice of pork. "Would you pass me the gravy and lima beans, Chet?"

"You know, Marine, it is a shame that Drake cannot be more involved here. He does have your best interest at heart." Chet handed Aunt Betsy the items.

"I know. But, you do understand, I don't believe him. I don't believe Ana-Geliza is so upset with me that she'd spend her every waking hour working out how to harm me. I mean, I'm a nobody. I'm not some head of state," Marine laughed. "At least, I don't think so. You know what I'm saying. I mean really. If Ana-Geliza is so dangerous, why is she spending her time trying to take me out?"

The Fire of Revenge

"Well, maybe, just maybe, Ana-Geliza is a crazy person. Crazy people do really weird things. Maybe you should do as Chet says. Let Drake help you more." Aunt Betsy got up and went into the kitchen.

Marine looked over at Chet. He was pushing his plate aside. She looked down at her plate and realized she'd hardly touched it.

Aunt Betsy walked back in with a red velvet cake topped with lemon and sour cream icing. It had become Marine's favorite after she tried it at her celebratory party. Where was the time going, she wondered.

* * * * *

After dinner, Marine helped clean up the dishes and the kitchen. She then went up to her room where she thought about what Chet and Aunt Betsy had said about Drake. She picked up the phone and dialed his hotel room.

"Drake, can you talk?"

"Yes. It's good to hear from you."

"Well, Chet and Aunt Betsy encouraged me to reconsider allowing you to do more for me as far as this Ana-Geliza thing is concerned."

"That's good to hear. May I come over?"

"Now?"

"Yes."

"No, not now. I've got some more things to work out. I'll be on evening shift for the next several days. So, would you like to meet tomorrow for lunch?"

"Sure. What time?"

"Let's meet around noon. I need to be at work at eight. We may need to include Aunt Betsy and Chet. Will that be a problem?"

"No. Where you want to meet?"

"There's a great Chinese restaurant in town—Peking. Have you been there?"

"No. Sounds like a good idea. I'm looking forward to seeing you."

"Drake, I don't want you to get the wrong idea."

"I'm not expecting anything. I'll see you at noon."

"Sounds like a plan. See ya."

"Good night."

"Good night, Drake."

As Marine hung up the phone, she played with the corner of her journal lying on the table next to her bed. Flipping the edges, she thought about Ana-Geliza. *What am I going to do?* She picked up her journal, sat on the side of her bed, and began to write. She had learned that writing her thoughts down helped her weigh the pros and cons of what she needed to do versus what she wanted to do. Right now, she had no idea.

As she wrote, she kept thinking about Drake and how she must have known him before she lost her memory. Her flashbacks were coming more frequently, yet she couldn't quite figure out how or when she first met Drake.

As she rested her head back, a memory of playing with a group of little girls in a schoolyard somewhere in a city came to her. She could see a woman off to one side. The woman held a switch or stick of some kind in her hand. A shiny, black car pulled up and stopped beside the curb. A woman got out. Her long, black coat, a hat that covered her face and high heels portrayed an aura of elegance. Marine watched her walk over to the other lady. As she did, the sun's rays seemed to glisten off her coat.

She rose up and rubbed her head. That memory was stronger than the others were, she thought.

TWELVE

RENEWED ENCOUNTER

Lunch was stressful for Marine. Chet and Aunt Betsy couldn't join her and Drake at the restaurant. The idea of spending all of her time alone with Drake had put her on edge. She had barely touched her food.

"Okay. I give up." Drake put his chopsticks down. "What gives with you?"

Marine looked up and smiled, "What?"

"We've sat here for almost thirty minutes. You've barely touched your food, and you seem to be miles away. You haven't said five words to me. What's wrong?"

"I don't know what you're talking about. I'm trying to be—"

"What? You're not trying to tell me that you're being a good date, are you?"

Marine winked at Drake. "Sure, why not?"

"That is about the—"

"Well, Hello Drake and Marine! How are you guys? Fancy seeing you in New Brook," the man said.

Drake looked at Marine, and she looked at the man. A memory formed of her with Drake on a sailboat in the Caribbean.

"Well, hello!" Drake said as he stood and offered his hand. "Marine, you remember Connie and Martin Thomas, don't you? They took us on the lovely evening cruise when we were in Antigua."

Marine tried to swallow her food. She was stunned at her memory and that night's events came rushing back to her.

"Oh. Hello," Marine tried to stand.

"No need to get up," Martin said. "Connie thought that it was the two of you over here. We don't mean to interrupt your lunch. We did want to introduce you to Connie's brother, Jerry Cline and his fiancée, Peggy Westbon. How long will you be in New Brook? We'd love to hook up with you guys. We had such a good time on our boat."

"Well, we're not sure how long I'll be in town. Marine lives here now. She is a

The Fire of Revenge

firefighter for Chestnut Mountain Station Three."

"You've got to be kidding me," Jerry spoke up. "I'm a firefighter for Salem Station One. How long have you been on the job?"

"A little more than two weeks now. I finished The Academy and went straight to work. I pull my first night shift tonight."

"You guys have been having it rough the last two evenings on night shift. We've had a rash of car fires and some recent warehouse fires, too."

"How long have you been with the department?"

"Twenty years."

"You've seen a lot then."

"Yes. That I have. What is your last name?"

"Letsco."

"You aren't the recent Academy Leader Letsco the Battalion Chiefs are all buzzing about, are you?"

Marine blushed.

Drake spoke up, "Yes, she is. What have you heard?"

"Oh, nothing much. Just that she broke every record you could set while going through The Academy. And to be a woman, too." Jerry stuck out his hand. "It's a pleasure to meet you."

Marine shook his hand. "Thank you, Jerry. It is a pleasure meeting all of you. I hate to cut this short, but I do need to get some things done before I have to report to work later this evening. It was nice of you to stop by and remind us of our time in the Caribbean."

"Yes, it was nice," Drake said. "But, before you go, are you guys going to be in the area awhile?"

"Yes," Connie said. "We sailed up to the North Carolina coast and docked our boat there. We plan to go back in late spring. We spend the winter season here. We should plan to meet up for cards and drinks."

"That would be fun," Drake said and motioned to Marine to respond.

"Yes, we would like that," Marine stared at Drake as she continued, "I really hate to end making plans, but I do need to talk to Drake before I must leave."

"Oh, sure," Martin said. "We'll be in touch." They all turned to walk away when Jerry turned back.

"You be safe out there. I don't go on shift again until Monday."

The Fire of Revenge

"Thanks," Marine said. "See you."
She turned back to Drake.
"What the hell?"

THIRTEEN

....

IS IT DECEPTION?

Marine grabbed her coat and purse. "You can pay for the bill. And, while you're at it, you can figure out how you're going to explain keeping our relationship a secret all this time. How dare you look at me like that? You don't love me. If you did, you wouldn't have hidden that information." Marine stood up, put on her coat. "Right now, I could care less if I ever lay eyes on you again."

* * * * *

"How did your shift go?" Wayne said as he walked up to Marine at her locker. She continued to put the manuals she had been reading away. "You know you were lucky we didn't have many fire calls last night or this morning, far as that goes."

"Hi, Captain. Yes, I know. I was able to get in some reading on the equipment for the ladder truck. Fish showed me some things regarding the pumper, too."

"Have you finished your reading?"

"Yes, Sir."

"Letsco, I would like to plan to talk with you prior to the start of your next shift. Plan to report for duty thirty minutes early."

"Thanks, Captain." Marine watched as Wayne walked away. That was cold, she thought. Wayne had made it clear there were not to be any friendly actions toward him now that he was Captain. 'Oh Captain, My Captain.' Walt Whitman's words rang in her head. Picking up her coat, Marine figured the idea of having a relationship with him was something else she would have to get used to doing without. She walked out into the early morning air.

On her drive home, she began to think over the events of the previous day's lunch. She couldn't talk to Chet yet, Marine thought as she turned down the drive to Aunt Betsy's house. She needed to think through spending time

The Fire of Revenge

with Drake and Connie and Martin Thomas. Marine wondered what they knew about her. The fact she had a memory flashback while talking with them unnerved her a little. She parked the Jeep in the driveway and sat there thinking. "I don't *get* unnerved." She slammed her fist on the steering wheel.

* * * * *

"Hey, Marine," Aunt Betsy said. "I've got your breakfast ready for you."

"Thanks. But, I'm not hungry. I need to go take care of some things." Marine took the stairs two steps at a time. She couldn't talk to anyone, not yet. She had to figure out what was going on. Her memory was coming back faster than she was prepared to remember. She rubbed her head and went into the bathroom; she pulled out some aspirin and took four. There was a knock on her bedroom door.

"Marine, may I come in?"

"Can it wait?"

"Please?"

"Sure, Chet. Come on in." Marine went and sat in the chair next to her bed. "What's up?"

"Aunt Betsy is worried about you. Are you okay?"

"Yes. Why?"

"She thought maybe something was wrong. You did not stop and talk with her like you normally do. Has something happened?"

"You know it has."

"What?"

"Drake spoke to you."

"Why would you say that?"

"Chet, don't be coy with me. He told you we met up with Connie and Martin at the restaurant at lunch didn't he?"

"He did mention something about it. Are you okay?"

"No."

Chet took a seat on the side of the bed. "Want to talk?"

"No."

"Would it help if I tell you what I know?"

"No."

"Marine. Do not shut me out now. Did you have a memory flashback?"

"What if I did?"

"I am your doctor. It is my job to help you."

"Now is not the time, Chet. I've got a lot of thinking to do."

Chet stood up. "Okay. I understand. But you need to hear the entire story before you—"

The Fire of Revenge

"Before what? Before I kill you?" Marine stood up and faced Chet squarely. "You are pushing me, Chet."

Chet backed away. "I will leave you alone. But, before I go."

"What?"

"Aunt Betsy wanted to see if you'd like to go out for a movie. What do I tell her?"

"I don't know." Marine stared at him and watched him close the door.

"What the hell am I doing?" She threw her journal against the wall. She threw herself on her bed. She just wanted to go to sleep and wake up to her world free of all trouble. She rolled over and looked up at the ceiling trying to think. What is all this about? The feeling of betrayal is heavy. Why? What is the point? Confusion was clouding her thinking.

Marine felt as though her head was going to explode. She thought about Wayne, Drake, Chet, and Aunt Betsy. Then, she thought about Ana-Geliza.

"What is her story?" she said to herself.

She walked over to the window. The morning sun began to break through the trees. No snow again, today. The sun felt warm on her arms. She thought about her time on the cruise ship. The last night when Ana-Geliza tried to kill her came rushing back.

"What was that all about?" she said, thinking aloud. It seemed no one was happy, yet everyone had an agenda. She wondered what Ana-Geliza's agenda was. Why was she after her? What does Chet know? How does Drake fit in? And, what about Wayne? Where did he *fit* into things? The only person that seemed to understand Marine was Aunt Betsy.

Marine got up and walked into her bathroom. She looked at her face in the mirror. Her eyes looked bloodshot. Anger had a way of stressing her face and twisting it into some kind of grotesque mask. As she splashed water over her eyes, she thought about how Aunt Betsy was her unwavering supporter.

She looked in her mirror and said, "I need to calm down. I don't need to take my anger and frustrations out on Aunt Betsy. She doesn't deserve that."

Marine went back to her bed and lay there thinking. She must have dozed off, as she was awakened by her alarm. She might as well go down and tell Chet and Aunt Betsy she'd like to go see a movie.

The Fire of Revenge

* * * * *

That afternoon when Chet, Aunt Betsy, and Marine walked out of the Millwald after watching *Into the Woods*, Marine thought she saw the back of someone she recognized. She shook it off to avoid dealing with it at that moment. Her imagination was working overtime.

"I don't know about you guys, but watching those folks around us eat that popcorn during the movie has made me hungry. Let's go have an early dinner before you have to report to work," Aunt Betsy said as she began to struggle putting on her coat.

"Sounds good to me. Where would you like to go?" Chet helped Aunt Betsy with her coat.

"I love the Matterhorn Restaurant and Lounge. Let's go there," Aunt Betsy said.

Marine slipped her arm into the crook of Chet's. "You can drive us, can't you? It sounds divine, Aunt Betsy."

"Sure. I will drive."

"It is divine. Marine, have you eaten there yet?"

"No, I haven't. The guys at the firehouse said they have a magnificent blue plate special."

"They do. And, the best part is that the lounge is part of the Wohlfahrt Haus Dinner Theatre. The main part of the building is where there are musical performances with a special dinner. Sometimes, at lunch, you can order the show food. It is my 'go-to' place for a good meal any day of the week, except of course on Monday," Aunt Betsy said as she got in the car.

"Why Monday?" Marine fixed her seat belt.

"I know this answer," Chet said as he started the car. "Most, if not all playhouses are dark on Mondays. It is the actors' weekend since so many shows are on Saturday and Sunday afternoon. There are those who believe it is based on superstition."

"That's interesting. I don't guess I ever thought about it before, but it makes sense."

As they drove the short distance to Wohlfahrt Haus, Marine thought back to the shadowy figure she saw. Could it have been Ana-Geliza? Really? After all this time? Why here? Why now?

Chet interrupted her thoughts. "We're here. Let's go get a seat."

"Hello, Betsy and Chet. It's good to see you. You can sit wherever you'd like."

The Fire of Revenge

"Hi, Suzi. Let's sit here." Aunt Betsy pointed to a booth near the fireplace. "Or, do you want to sit outside in the Bier Garten?"

"It's not too cold out today. The sun is bright. It almost feels like fall instead of the day before Christmas. Let's sit out there." Marine moved toward the side door. "Does this door lead outside?" Suzi nodded. "It will be nice to sit in the sun while we enjoy our meal."

"Suzi, have you met Marine?" Chet asked as he helped Aunt Betsy off with her coat.

Suzi extended a hand; Marine shook it. "Glad to meet you, Suzi."

"You, too. This is your first time here?"

"Yes. Aunt Betsy had mentioned it before."

"Do you live here?"

"I do, now. I'm actually thinking of finding my own place. Chet and Aunt Betsy have been kind enough to provide me a place, but it's time for me to move on." Marine looked at Chet to see what he would say. She hoped he would approve. She had not mentioned her idea of moving to either of them.

"Suzi, do you know of any rentals around? You help with placing the theatre's traveling actors. You might know someone we should contact for renting a small house." Aunt Betsy winked at Marine.

She was not surprised Aunt Betsy would join right in with her idea.

"Well, I actually don't do that part of the planning, but I know people that do. Let me think about it, and I'll get back to you. Here are your menus. What would you like to drink?"

"I hate to say this, but I think it is colder out here than I thought. May we move back in?" Aunt Betsy picked up her coat and walked away from the table.

"Sure. You can sit inside wherever you like. I don't mind."

"You see why I love this place," Aunt Betsy lead the way back inside. "Let's sit here near the fireplace. Brrr, there is a definite chill in the air, even with the sun shining."

"You folks settle in. I'll go see what I have left of our mulled cider. We had some earlier as we had a little celebratory party for Christmas Eve."

"Oh, I forgot all about your Christmas show. I so wanted to come see it. It is one of my favorite musicals." Aunt Betsy opened up her menu and began to scan the choices.

The Fire of Revenge

Suzi came back carrying three warm ciders. She placed them down and asked if they were ready to order. After each of them had made their selection, Suzi said, "Now remember, our Christmas show plays through the holidays until the final matinee on New Year's Eve. It sells out fast, so you should see if you can get tickets while you're here."

"You know, Marine, we have to plan to come one night. I love their food here."

"You know, I never would have thought there would be a German restaurant here. Why is that?"

"The owner built this dinner theatre in honor of her family and its German heritage. It has been here about fifteen years and has established a good following. We are lucky to have such an unusual venue here." Aunt Betsy reached for a sweetener to flavor her mulled cider.

"Why don't we eat here more often?" Marine said as she looked around at the décor. The bar area was highlighted in red with wood trim. The alpine look was adorned with Christmas decorations in celebration of the holiday season. "It's hard to believe Christmas is upon us already."

"You need to ask Chet why we don't eat here more often. I'd love more days off from cooking."

Suzi brought a plate of cheese and crackers. "Will you want something different to drink with your meal?"

Chet and Marine ordered hot tea while Aunt Betsy ordered water with lemon.

"Marine, how long will you be on evening shift?" Aunt Betsy said as she dipped a cracker into the soft cheese spread. "We need to plan our Christmas meal."

"One more day, and then I'll be scheduled to be off for four. But, things can change."

"Why do you say?" Chet asked as he took a bite of a cracker piled with cheese.

"We've been having a series of arson fires. At this point, we're not sure, if it is by a single arsonist or if it is a group of them. There are car fires that seem to be random and house fires, as well as businesses. The Captain and a few others are thinking there is someone out there trying to make a name for himself."

"Four days. And yes, I'm changing the subject. We should plan to come here for dinner one night. What else will you do with yourself?"

The Fire of Revenge

"I like that idea. And, I plan on using my time to look for a place." Marine reached for a cracker and cheese. "I better eat some of these before Chet eats it all. Aunt Betsy, I know you have said I don't need to move out. But, I think it is best. Besides, I need to start moving on with my life now that I'm working steadily."

"Marine, Drake and I discussed the need for you to stay where you are. We need to —"

Suzi walked up with the food. While she positioned the plates on the table, Marine wondered about sharing her memory flashbacks. To see the look on Chet's face might be interesting. The Matterhorn wasn't the place. Besides, she didn't want to upset Aunt Betsy. Marine was angry enough after she saw Connie and Martin Thomas. The memory flashbacks seconds after meeting them gave her pause when she realized she and Drake had been more intimate than she realized.

The two TVs in the bar showed a soccer game being played in Mexico. She watched to take her mind off her anger. It was hard to tell which team was which—the closed captioning was off, and the sound was down low. Marine tried to occupy her mind, but she found she kept wondering what Chet knew. The thought that Chet might know more about her past than he let on was not sitting well with her. Why was he so interested in her working so closely with Drake? If he didn't know anything, why would he keep encouraging her to work with him? It was becoming apparent to her that Drake and Chet might be conspirators.

* * * * *

As Chet pulled into the driveway of Aunt Betsy's home, Marine turned to him and said, "Are you coming in or are you going to head back to your house?"

"Actually, I was wondering if you would be interested in riding with me back to The Edith. I thought we should sit down with Drake and talk. Besides, Drake said he has something he needs to give you. He said that he forgot it when the two of you had lunch."

"Really? Drake told you that? Well, I would like to talk with you. I'd prefer to not talk with Drake around. Besides, I've got to get into my uniform first."

"Whether you come in or go on, Chet, before you talk with Marine, I'll need ten minutes with her. There is something I need to say—woman to woman. You understand?" Aunt Betsy got out of Chet's car.

Chet leaned out of his driver's side window, "Sure."

"Marine, why don't you meet Chet at The Edith? He can go ahead and let Drake know you're coming by. It's only a little after four. You won't be late for work. You can change, talk with me, and then head over to The Edith. You can go on to your shift from there."

Marine smiled at Aunt Betsy. She wasn't sure why, but she felt compelled to go along with Aunt Betsy's lead.

Marine turned to Chet, "You go on ahead. I'll meet you and Drake at The Edith. I'll only have about thirty minutes with you—I need to report to work early tonight."

Aunt Betsy walked Marine up to the house while Chet backed out of the driveway.

Marine stopped midstride, turned to Aunt Betsy, and said, "What's going on?"

FOURTEEN

A MARK REVEALED

Aunt Betsy slipped her hand into the crook of Marine's arm and guided her up the steps to the front porch. "Let's sit here and talk, shall we?" Aunt Betsy said. She took off her hat as she sat down in her rocking chair. "It's a little chilly, but what I'm about to tell you may cause you to heat up. I think you'll need some fresh air to keep yourself cool."

Marine pulled a chair closer, sat down, and looked at Aunt Betsy. "What can you possibly tell me that would cause me to get angry?"

"For one, you need to know that I know more about you than you know about yourself. And, for another, I'm not at all who Chet thinks I am. Or, I guess I should say who I *was*."

Marine stared at Aunt Betsy and nodded signaling her to continue.

"Let it be enough for me to tell you that I understand your past. I know who you are and when Chet learns about your past—" She paused, coughed a little, and then said, "Let's just say, he won't be able to handle it too well. He has a vision of you as a woman in distress. He is pleased he was able to help you. You are getting your memory back, aren't you?"

Marine nodded. "How—?"

"I've seen those in the field lose their memories because of injury. I've seen them gain them back. It is a shock. I need you to listen to me and I need you to believe what I'm about to say. It can mean your future. It will mean your life."

Marine adjusted her seat. "I am not sure I'm ready. I mean, I have had some flashbacks, but I'm having trouble believing what seems to be my reality. How could I—"

Aunt Betsy took Marine's hands in hers. "Don't worry about what you were or what you're going to learn about yourself and your past. Don't worry about what you're going to get; be happy for what you have; wish for what you want. Do you understand?"

The Fire of Revenge

Marine looked down at their hands intertwined. She noticed a mark on Aunt Betsy's hand, near the webbing between her forefinger and thumb she had not noticed before.

Aunt Betsy covered her hand with Marine's hand, and then smiled.

Marine nodded understanding.

FIFTEEN

....

FIRE ONE

Marine put on her newly starched and pressed navy blue uniform. She studied how she looked in the mirror. It seemed strange reading her last name backwards. The fire department patch had been stitched perfectly in place at her shoulder. Seeing her name embroidered in gold above the right breast pocket was what kept her turning to view it. She was a firefighter. She seemed to never tire of the idea. After her talk with Aunt Betsy, she felt relaxed. She wasn't as angry. She even felt good about her chosen path. She would no longer look to her past; she was going to look forward from now on. She nodded to her image in the mirror and silently whispered, "I am performing a service."

"Marine?" Aunt Betsy called upstairs.

"Yes, Aunt Betsy," Marine said as she walked to the top of the stairs. "Am I late?"

"Remember, Chet is waiting for you at The Edith. You better get going or you won't have time for that talk with him and Drake. You probably should have left ten minutes ago."

"I'll be right down."

Marine picked up her issued hat and jacket. It was official as far as she was concerned. *Drake and Chet can play their stupid games with Ana-Geliza. As for me, I'm going to focus on being Firefighter Letsco.*

* * * * *

Standing before Drake's room at The Edith, Marine paused for a moment. She thought about turning around and leaving, when the door opened.

"What's the matter now?" Drake said as he motioned for Marine to step through the door.

"You sure know how to piss a girl off."

"What, what did *I* do?"

"You know exactly what you did. Where do you get off telling Chet that we had met up with the Thomases? Where did that come from?"

"It came from the fact that I want to keep you safe. I want to protect you."

"From who? Ana-Geliza?"

"Yes!"

"Well, guess what Mr. Spy? She's here in town."

"I know."

If Marine were driving, she would have slammed on the brakes so Drake would have been thrown through the window. As it was, she hit him so hard he fell on his bed.

"Merry Christmas!"

"Damn, Marine. You've got one hell of a sucker punch. Chill out."

"Chill out! What do you mean you know she's here? How long have you known? When were you going to tell me?" Marine looked at Chet, who had not left his seat.

"Do not look at me. He did not tell me that Ana-Geliza was here."

"Well, what has he told you, Chet? How long have the two of you been in cahoots? And don't you dare tell me you haven't been. It's bloody obvious." Marine stomped over to the window.

"I would not stand near that window," Chet said as he offered Marine his seat. "Sit here."

"I haven't told you because we haven't had an opportunity to be alone to talk. I wasn't sure where she was when we were last here. So, I didn't say anything then. But, this evening, while you were out, I caught a glimpse of her. Then, when Chet came here a little while ago, I saw her again, this time through that window. She was down on the sidewalk looking up in this direction."

"You saw her, too?" Marine looked at Chet.

Chet nodded. He was acting as though he was afraid to speak.

"Has the cat got your tongue, Chet?" Marine asked.

"No," Drake answered. "He is probably staying out of our discussion to cut down on any confusion."

"Confusion. You mean the two of you have a plan and you hope to trick me into following. Well, you can think differently. I realize what's going on here now. Chet, how long have you been working with Drake?"

"I am not working *with* Drake. He confided in me when we were on the ship that Ana-Geliza was trying to kill you. He told me in confidence in order that I might be able to help keep you safe."

The Fire of Revenge

Drake stood up and walked over to Marine. "What do you mean you saw her? When? Where?"

"Yeah. I saw her. Today was the third time. She is always in the shadows. This last time, I caught a glimpse of her back. But, I'd know that walk anywhere. She was walking away from the movie theatre. Why?"

"What?" Chet stood up. "You would know her walk anywhere? Does this mean you are having memory flashbacks? Are you remembering your experiences with Ana-Geliza in the past?"

"Slow down, Chet," Drake said as he turned toward Marine. "This isn't good. She must've known you would be there. She staged it. Ana-Geliza would not have made herself known unless she was ready to let you know. She has a plan."

"Chet, to answer your questions. Yes and no." She turned to Drake, "Tell me something."

"Okay, what?"

"The card you handed me the other day said special intelligence. I didn't dig deeper. I've since decided to ask. Are you what I've heard refer to as MI6?"

"Yes."

"How'd you know me?"

"I met you on the ship."

"Did we have a relationship before I lost my memory?"

There was a long silence.

"Drake?"

No response.

"Drake, I am starting to remember things. I know we were on the sailboat with Connie and Martin. I know our night together was not platonic. I know my past is more complicated than I imagined."

Marine turned to Chet.

"And, Doc, despite your efforts to convince me that all those stories I've shared were dreams, I'm pretty sure they weren't. I've been living a deceptive life. I'm not any better than any crook out there. I've been keeping secrets, too. Yes, like the two of you. My memory is coming back. I'll tell you one thing; I don't like what I see in my head."

"Marine," Chet said as he walked to her chair. "I did what I needed to do in order to give you time to gain strength. Learning about your past is not an easy thing no matter what it is. Drake had told me you worked for a government agency. He didn't tell me anything more. I think I should leave the two of you to talk this out. Marine, you and I can talk in the morning when you get off shift."

Chet grabbed his coat and closed the door behind him.

Marine looked at Drake, "Well, he sure knows how to make a quick exit. What gives with you two anyway?"

"Let's not worry about him right now. What's important is that you realize I am here to help protect you. How did you know I was MI6?"

"It came to me when we were talking with Connie and Martin. You knew me before the cruise, didn't you?"

Drake smiled. He walked over toward Marine and looked as though he was going to speak, but instead, he reached down and pulled Marine up out of the chair and into his arms.

His breathing was rushed. "Drake?"

"I can't do this anymore, Marine. I've got to have you. I love you. Do you understand? I love you."

* * * * *

Sergeant George "Fish" Fisher, Marine's FTO, walked up to her locker. "Letsco, it's time that we do what we call 'a walk through a fire truck.' You'll show me what you know about the tools and equipment that you've been using these last few weeks."

Marine turned her head sideways to look out of her locker, "Now?"

"Yes. I'll meet you there in five."

Marine finished storing her coat and personal items, closed up her locker and walked out to the bays. Fish was standing near a fire truck in the center bay.

"Letsco, this is fire engine twenty-seven, a three-year-old Pierce with a 1250 gallon per minute pump that carries one thousand gallons of water." Marine looked over the massive machine and marveled at all of the different parts and fixtures. "As you have already learned, everything you see on this truck—every little bolt, every chrome piece—has a use and function. Right now, it is your job to tell me what each of those little knobs, gadgets, and gauges are—what they do and how each works. Capiche?"

Marine studied his face. He looked like he had been fighting fires a long time. His eyes sparkled with pride.

The Fire of Revenge

Fish continued with Marine's test by opening up various compartments and asking her to explain what each contained along with proper names and uses. After about thirty minutes, Marine's brain was reeling.

She decided to have a little fun with Fish. "The Pressure Principle Two states that pressure applied on a confined liquid from an external source will be transmitted equally in all directions through the liquid without a reduction in magnitude. This principle explains what?"

Fish looked at her as though she had two heads. "Damn, —"

Fish was interrupted by the sound of loud varying tones.

"Station Three – Structure fire at 1275 Community Heights; cross streets Malin and Spring – heavy smoke showing – 18:30," the intercom crackled.

"Letsco, get your gear and get your ass on the truck."

Bodies were moving all around Marine as she heard someone yell, "Fish, are you coming?"

"Yeah. I've gotta wait on the FNG."

Marine grabbed her gear and made a beeline for the engine. She crawled up into the six-man cab. She had about half of her gear on as she managed to get herself buckled in when the pumper pulled out. She reached into her pants pocket to make sure she had her coin. It was there right where she had put it.

Fish tried to help her finish putting on her gear while the other guys looked on.

"What's FNG?"

"Freaking New Girl. That's you. Your official nickname."

"I thought it was Probie."

"Nah. That's for anyone new. You, on the other hand, are special."

The rest of the cab broke into laughter.

* * * * *

The ladder truck pulled up to the scene behind the engine pumper with sirens blaring. Marine leaned over to Fish, "I hadn't seen Roy drive like that before. What's with him? I mean, he blew through the intersections and people seemed to know to get out of his way."

Fish shook his head, leaned forward, and yelled above the noise, "Both vehicles are equipped with a Federal siren. It is specially designed to send out a warning sound as much as a mile away depending on the height of surrounding structures and the wind. When we get out, you stay with me like glue. If I run, you better keep up."

Roy pulled up to the curb in front of the house. Everyone began to move out. Each firefighter had his assigned duty and very little was said. Marine noted that the shift worked with the efficiency of a pit crew at an NASCAR race. She wondered if she would ever feel a part of their team. She still felt new, the Freaking New Girl; she laughed under her breath.

Once the engine pumper was set up and the hose was charged, LT called for the initial attack team.

"That's us," Fish called to Marine.

They entered the house to begin fighting the fire while firefighters Crab and Willie stayed back.

"They'll be our backup until needed for relief or help," Fish yelled to Marine. She could hear through her lapel mic as LT commanded the scene from the front yard where she saw him standing when they went into the house. He told Cotton Top and Doc to stand by at the ladder truck. Roy was working the pumper. She wasn't sure where Captain Wayne was, but he was probably observing.

At first, Marine couldn't see a thing. She held the hose tight. The smoke was blacker and denser than any she had seen at The Academy. She wasn't sure if what she was doing was helping, but she wasn't going to let go of the hose to find out.

It seemed as quick as they went into the house that the smoke turned from black to white and they were back out.

Fish walked up to LT. "Lieutenant, we've knocked the fire down. We've got a fatality. We probably need to get the Fire Marshal here and the ME."

"Where was the fatality?"

"It was in a back bedroom. The body was an adult."

Fish turned to Marine after completing his report to LT. "Way to go, FNG. Your first fire fatality. We'll be here a while. Since we were the responding company, we have to maintain custody of the property until the Fire Marshal and the ME arrive. You do know what an ME is, don't you?"

The Fire of Revenge

"Yes. The medical examiner. I do have a question or two?"

"Shoot."

"Why do you use ME for the medical examiner, but don't use FM for fire marshal?"

"That's easy. FM is a radio frequency. What's your second question?"

"How long will you guys keep calling me FNG?"

"You've forgotten already. You'll be Probie until a new firefighter comes on shift or you get promoted. But, you'll always be FNG. Merry Christmas."

Marine looked over at the pumper longing to head back to the firehouse. Her feet were tired.

"Don't get any ideas about heading back to the firehouse. We'll have to wait until the ME's and Fire Marshal's work is finished before we can go back in and walk the scene."

* * * * *

An hour passed.

Fish walked over to Marine. "The Fire Marshal brought two of his Deputy Fire Marshals with him, so things got wrapped up relatively quick. They and the ME cleared us to go in. You ready to go walk your first fatal fire scene?"

Marine nodded. She was glad they had already taken the body away. She wasn't sure she was ready to see the remains up close. Fish had stopped her when he saw the body earlier. She was glad. With the memory flashbacks and dreams she'd been having, she wondered how she would have reacted. She followed Fish over to the engine.

Fish handed Marine a helmet, "We will be going inside a fire scene that has been worked, but we still have to wear our turnout gear. You do not need to wear an air pack. We keep these helmets loose for just such an occasion. Now, follow me closely, and I will point a few obvious things out to you as we go."

She put on her helmet, leaving the facemask up. She felt a little giddy at the idea of what she was about to see. She had spent fourteen weeks reading about fire scenes. Finally, to get to see an actual fire scene was exciting. Yet, she found herself feeling torn about the fact that someone died.

Fish stopped and turned to her. "Who lives here?"

Marine said, "I don't know."

The Fire of Revenge

"Your answer should be nobody. This is one of the things you need to learn to notice. The electric meter had been pulled. No one should have been in this house. It should have been vacant."

"How did you know that?"

Fish pointed to the side of the house. She could see the spot where a meter would be if a house had been legally occupied.

"I saw the meter had been pulled as we drove up to the scene. You need to learn to look for these kinds of things from the second you begin to arrive at a fire. These kinds of details will help you size up a scene, and it can help you save the life of your fellow firefighters, not to mention yourself."

Marine pondered his words. She realized that fighting a fire didn't start when you walked into a burning building. It began much earlier—in preparation.

Fish and Marine continued to walk through the house, when they turned down the hallway, Marine could see streaks of black soot on the walls.

"Do you know what that smell is?"

"Burnt flesh," Marine said without thinking.

"Very good, Letsco. How'd you know that?"

"I don't know." Marine could see the nightclub where the bodies had burned.

"Letsco, didn't I tell you to stick with me?"

"Yes, sir." She walked up to where Fish was standing at the entrance to a bedroom. She had lagged behind while thinking about the nightclub fire. She shook off a feeling of dread that came over her as she looked around the bedroom.

"The walls will tell you a lot about what went on here. Look at them."

Marine stepped into the room and began to look at each of the four walls.

"What do you see?" Before she could answer, Fish said, "Let me explain what you see. First, there is graffiti on the walls. Most of it is gang graffiti. This could be a gang hangout, drug house, anything. Second, the construction of the walls tells me this house was built in the forties. You can tell by the plaster on the walls. Next, you can tell by the smoke patterns and burn patterns where the fire originated and the intensity of the fire. When you know what to look for, these things will piece together the story of what happened here."

The Fire of Revenge

Looking at the wall, Marine noticed some patterns. One, in particular, looked familiar, but she decided it was part of the graffiti.

"Do you see the area that is not burned?" Marine nodded. "That is where the body laid and it took all the flame. The body protected the floor from the fire, so it was not charred."

As they walked back out to the engine, Marine thought about how eager she was to learn about firefighting and how it was tempered by the loss of a life. She wondered whose daughter or son the victim was. She wondered if she or he would be missed.

After the shift had arrived back at the station, they finished cleaning the tools and equipment; then they were called into the firehouse kitchen.

Fish pulled out a chair, "Letsco, I know you've been here before. But, this fire is a little different due to the fatality. We'll meet in here for the last half hour of our shift for a call debrief. You need to listen. You need to pay attention. But most importantly, you need to remember what this sign here says."

Marine looked at the wall and read what she saw out loud:

What you SEE here, What you HEAR here, What you SAY here... When you LEAVE here LET IT STAY HERE!

Marine turned around and saw that all the members of C Shift were seated around the kitchen table. Captain Wayne walked in and sat at the head of the table. Marine sat down beside Fish.

Fish turned to Marine. "The most important point of this exercise is to go over the call. As we've done before, we've come back here and talked about each fire. This time, we'll all go over what you did wrong, whether you did it or not. We'll sit here and break your balls."

"Break my balls? I don't have balls."

"Letsco, it's a figure of speech. At this rate, you'll hold the rank of Probie even after a new person comes along or you get promoted." Fish punched her shoulder. "Seriously, Marine. It's part of the tradition of the department. When we're at a fire, I'm dependent on you, you're dependent on me; we both want to go home when we're done. So, the breaking of the balls is a way to learn where a Probie is—what is she

The Fire of Revenge

made of. Can she get involved and take the abuse? We need to know so that when we're in the throes of a bad call—a deadly fire, as we had tonight—we are sure that you will hold up your end of the job.

Marine nodded as she looked around the room. "So, will it hurt?"

"No, not physically, but it does get serious. The serious part comes when we talk to each other about what we each did at a fire because everything is about bringing the Probie up. This is all for you, Letsco."

Marine reached into her pocket and pulled out her commemorative coin from her graduation. She began to use it as a lucky coin, rubbing it with her fingers as they began to break her balls.

* * * * *

The shift ended. The drive home was somber. Chet and Aunt Betsy were up when Marine walked through the door. It was eight thirty, Christmas morning.

"Would you like some breakfast before you take a shower and go to bed?" Aunt Betsy handed Marine a cup of coffee. "Merry Christmas, Dear."

"Merry Christmas. I don't think so. It was a rough night. You'll hear on today's news that we had a fatality."

"Oh dear," Aunt Betsy hugged Marine. "Are you okay?"

"Yes, I'm tired."

"You go on up. Get a shower and rest. We can talk when you wake up a little later. What time would you like to be awakened? I'd like to have our Christmas dinner this evening around five. Will that work?"

"Yes. It will be nice to have a quiet, restful visit with you this evening. I must report at eight. That should be fine. Wake me up at two. I would like to talk to you, Chet."

"Okay." She went upstairs.

In her room, Marine stripped off her uniform, got a shower. As the water flowed over her, she thought about her day. It had been full. She still wasn't entirely over her anger at Chet and Drake, but the fire scene had tempered it.

While lounging on her bed she looked at her tattoo. In her journal, she drew an outline of the pattern and thought about what she had seen on the wall of the bedroom at the house fire.

SIXTEEN

CHRISTMAS DAY

Marine heard a knock on her door. "Are you awake?" the voice called from the other side. She could hear rain patting the windowsill.

After looking at the clock, she wondered why so early.

"Yes." She choked as she cleared her throat. "Yes, I am. Why?"

"You said you wanted to be awakened at two. You said you wanted to talk to me. Can I come in?" Marine came out of her stupor and realized Chet was talking.

"Oh gees, Chet. It's still Thursday, isn't it. It's Christmas! Give me a sec and you can come on in." She pulled the covers up around her neck and leaned against the headboard making it snap against the wall. Annoyed by the sound, she got up, threw on a sweatshirt and her jeans. She sat on the window seat.

"Come on in, Chet. I'm ready."

Chet walked in. He pulled up a chair beside her. "I guess you want to talk about the death?"

"Actually, I want to talk about what I saw after the body was removed." She pulled her pants leg up and pointed to her tattoo.

Chet looked at her with a quizzical eye. "You saw another tattoo like yours on the body?"

"I just told you the body had been removed. They didn't allow me to see the body. Fish said everyone had to be pulled out when they realized there was a fatality to keep everyone from stomping on evidence. So, I never got a close look. But, you know, I did see this pattern on the wall near some graffiti. It could be a coincidence. What do you think?"

"I don't know."

"As much as I hate to admit it and as mad as I've been, you might be right that I need to keep Drake informed. After seeing Ana-Geliza several times and now this, I'm not sure what to think."

"Why did you not tell me before about Ana-Geliza?"

"I thought my eyes were playing tricks on me. Both times, it was in a fleeting glimpse. Kind of like you might think a shadow passed by—you turn and realize it was nothing." Marine saw Chet's look of concern. "What? Okay, I get it. I was scared."

"Scared of me?"

"No, of you telling me I couldn't go ahead with becoming a firefighter."

"Marine, if I thought you could not handle it, I never would have suggested you look for a job. It is imperative you keep me informed from now on. Okay?"

"Sure. I'll do that, Chet. I don't see why you're getting all huffy. It couldn't have been her."

"Have you kept anything else from me?"

"No. No, I haven't."

Chet got up, moved the chair back to the desk. "Just know that I do have your best interest at heart. Now, get dressed for work. Aunt Betsy has fixed you a lovely Christmas dinner."

"Thanks, Chet. I'll be down soon."

* * * * *

The dinner was like it had been pulled off the pages of an elaborate home magazine. The table was decorated to perfection and at each place setting was a Christmas decoration. Aunt Betsy was dressed in her best dress and Chet was in a suit. Marine blushed.

"Oh. I didn't dress appropriately. I'm in my work clothes. Give me five minutes."

She ran to her room and changed into one of the dresses she had in her bag from the cruise. As she put it on, a splitting headache came over her. She managed to make it to the bathroom, where she took a couple of headache pills. She took a washcloth, wet it, and placed on her forehead and lay down on the bed.

"Marine? Are you okay?" Aunt Betsy came in.

"Yes. I got a horrible headache. I had to lie down."

"How are you now?"

"I'm better. Will you zip me up?"

"Sure. Don't you look lovely. Well, my, my, my. I did not know you had such beautiful studs."

Marine blushed, looked in the mirror, and saw the five sparkling round cut diamond studs pierced in her chest.

The Fire of Revenge

"I have no idea why I did that. But, there they are." The navy blue sequin dress with its scooped neck set the five studs off with perfection.

"Let's go have dinner," Aunt Betsy said as she helped Marine out the door. When they started down the stairs, Marine turned, pointed to her feet, and began to laugh. Marine still had on her work boots.

"Come on, you don't need to change. I think it looks very becoming."

Chet had finished setting the food on the table. Marine stood in awe as she looked at all of the dishes from lamb to country ham. There were three different types of salads, an asparagus casserole, a sweet potato casserole, and a gravy boat. Homemade rolls with honey butter finished out the table setting.

"If you tell me you have more than one dessert, I think I will pop. I do have to work tonight," Marine said as she piled her plate high.

Through most of the dinner, there was very little talking except to ask someone to pass a dish or hand a roll. Finally, it came time to get up from the table.

"Aunt Betsy, you have truly outdone yourself. This is by far the best meal I have ever enjoyed eating." Marine walked over to her and hugged her. "Thank you for the best Christmas I have ever had."

Aunt Betsy hugged Marine back and kissed her on the cheek. "Now for presents. Let's go in the den and we can enjoy our dessert with a hot mulled cider afterward. Okay?"

"Sounds perfect," Chet said.

They exchanged their packages and each sat in a different location of the room around the tree. They agreed to open their presents together.

Aunt Betsy and Chet explained that they always bought each other something for their hobbies. Aunt Betsy presented Chet some ammunition for his guns while Chet gave Aunt Betsy some yarn for her knitting and crocheting.

Marine gave Chet a rare collector's book on the Civil War. He was ecstatic. He gave Marine a gift certificate to the local Williams-Sonoma kitchen store to help her start her new apartment or house when she planned to move.

The Fire of Revenge

"Chet, this is so thoughtful of you. It makes me want to cry to think you are okay with me getting my own place."

"You're welcome, Marine. I think you need to do what makes you happy."

"Okay, Aunt Betsy, here's yours."

Aunt Betsy opened her gift from Marine; it was a gift certificate to the local garden shop inside a pair of leather garden gloves.

"Oh, my. These gloves are perfect. Spring will be here before we know it. Okay. You open yours now."

Marine was hesitant. For some reason, she felt she would cry. The box was wrapped in delicate tissue paper and a big red bow. She opened it and found a velveteen case. Inside was a beautiful, old pin. It was rimmed with garnet stones, and in the center was a small yellow cameo. Marine gasped.

"Are you okay?"

"Yes. It is just too beautiful. I have always loved cameo pins."

"Really?" Chet leaned forward.

"Yes. I don't know why I thought that."

Aunt Betsy smiled. "Do you like it?"

"Yes. It is lovely. I will cherish it always."

"I hope you do. It belonged to my mother."

SEVENTEEN

....

FIRE TWO

Marine arrived at the firehouse with about five minutes to spare. Fighting the fire, the previous night, had taken more out of her than her experiences at The Academy. She took a huge breath, grabbed her stuff from her car, and walked inside. At her locker, she began to look over her turnout gear. Her mind kept wandering back to the mark she'd seen at the fire scene.

"Letsco, Merry Christmas!" She turned to see Sergeant Roy.

"Merry Christmas, Roy."

"Give me a hug, girl." They hugged.

"You are looking serious. You're not having second thoughts before you even have a few fires under your belt, are ya?"

"No. Actually, I was wondering about last night's fire scene."

"You did good. You knew what you had to do, and you did it. I mean, how many people do you know who think it is okay to walk into a burning building? Most people say, 'We gotta go that-a-way,'" Roy said as he pointed behind him. Marine smiled. "You see. Even you realize the craziness of it."

"When I did the walk through with Fish, I saw things I never saw during the actual fire."

"Talk to some of the guys and let them share their stories—the things they've seen. We've all had them."

"You too?"

"Me, too."

Just then, the speakers blared out a fire call. We were being paged for another fire.

"Station Three – Structure fire at 7135 Jefferson Avenue; cross streets 30th and 32nd – fully involved; threatening other structures – 20:25."

This time, Marine was in the pumper with her turnout gear on and strapped in by the time Fish joined her. She had already made sure her coin was in her pocket.

The Fire of Revenge

"Well, look at you, FNG," Fish said as he stepped up into the cab. "You got it wrong. You're going in the ladder truck this time. Captain is riding here. Head over there and be quick about it."

Marine hopped out and made her way over to the ladder truck. The one time she beat Fish to the pumper and she was in the wrong vehicle. She shook her head as she got up in the cab.

"Welcome, FNG." Crab called as he slammed the back cab door behind her and got up in the truck. "You're going to love riding with me." Crab pulled the truck out onto the main road behind the engine as they rolled out.

* * * * *

The ride took about seven minutes, and along the way, jokes were flying. It was part of the ritual of heading toward a fire.

Cotton Top leaned forward and shouted, "FNG, do you know why they have Dalmatian dogs on fire trucks?" Marine saw him jab Willie.

"For good luck?"

"No, to find the fire hydrants." Cotton Top and Willie chuckled. Doc shook his head.

Willie retorted, "FNG, why doesn't the fire chief look out the window in the morning?"

"I don't have a clue."

"They wouldn't have anything to do in the afternoon." This time, all chuckled. Marine realized then that though she thought Roy was the jokester of the shift, with these guys, she was learning *they* were the pranksters.

Doc said to Marine, "Don't mind them. They're just having some fun at your expense—breaking your balls, so to speak." Marine nodded. "You can relax fellas. I'm not sure, but the FNG might be scared of heights. Are you?"

Marine looked them over, smiled, and wondered how tough they were. She had a sudden flash of jumping from an exploding building. They had no idea what she could do, and as far as that goes, neither did *she*. Nodding to Doc that she was fine with heights, she wondered what their stories were.

As the ladder truck pulled up, Crab looked at Marine through the rearview mirror. "Looks like we're going to have exposure issues."

"What kind of issues?"

"The adjacent structures look like they are starting to smoke from the heat. This fire could get dangerous quick." Crab put on the brakes.

The Fire of Revenge

"Thanks, Crab. I hadn't thought of that."

"Letsco, there is a lot of tradition in the fire service," Doc said as he reached for his helmet. "You know why firemen wear red suspenders, don't ya?"

"No, I don't. Why?"

"To hold up their pants."

As they got out, they all shook their heads. Marine felt dumb for falling for such an old joke. She put the feeling aside as she knew she needed to get her head into working the fire.

Fish yelled to Marine, "You help Roy hook the pumper up to the hydrant. I'm heading over here. You stay with the engine when you're done."

She watched Fish put on his air pack. Then, he and Crab went into the structure while Willie and Cotton Top began to attack the fire from outside the flamed-covered building.

After about five minutes, Fish returned and spoke with LT; Crab joined the other two still fighting the fire. LT and Fish walked over toward Marine.

"The other building has not been breached. The knocking down of the fire is helping to cool that side of the building so we may be lucky at saving that one, but this building here is a loss," Fish said.

Just then, Marine noticed something near the area in between the buildings.

"Look," she said and ran toward the building.

Suddenly, she was knocked to the ground.

"Don't you ever do that again," Fish rolled Marine over on her back. "Are you crazy?"

"But—"

Marine pointed to a body.

* * * * *

Again, the Fire Marshal was called to the scene along with the ME. Three hours later, the shift was ready to return to the firehouse. By the time they got back, no one was cracking jokes. Each firefighter was dog-tired. It was a hot fire. The shed was lost, but the structure to the right of the building was saved. The body that was found had not suffered burns; so it was not clear if death was caused by smoke inhalation or something else. After the truck and engine had been staged at the firehouse, the shift worked at cleaning up the tools and equipment to prep for their next run. There was still no talking.

The Fire of Revenge

"Come on, FNG," Fish motioned for Marine to join him in the kitchen. "We'll be having a debrief here in five minutes. The Fire Marshal along with a Police Investigator will be joining us. You need to watch and listen. Okay?"

"You mean you don't want me asking questions?"

"You're getting smarter." Fish slapped Marine on the back. They walked over to the long kitchen table and took their seats. The rest of Shift C came in followed by Captain Wayne, the Fire Marshal, and a Police Investigator.

The Captain stood in front of the room, "Folks, this last one was bad. I'm turning this debrief over to Fire Marshal Matt Pike and Police Investigator Ralph Linkous."

"Thank you, Captain. You can see from the photos Investigator Linkous is passing around taken of both scenes from last night and this morning. We suspect that there may be a serial arsonist at work. After you've had time to review the photos, we'll interview each of you to determine if anyone saw anything unusual, out of place, or maybe even a suspect that you might have caught a glimpse of when pulling up to the scene."

The shift spent the next ten minutes looking over the photographs. When Marine had her chance, she gave out a muffled moan.

"Are you okay?" Crab said.

"Yeah." Marine smiled. "I'm fine."

"They call me Crab because sometimes I can be a hard nose, but you looked like you were shaken by that picture. It is not bad to be human. It is hard to see another human hurt."

"Crab, thank you. I'm okay." Marine looked down at the picture. It was there, as clear as if someone had circled it, and then put a large arrow pointing to it. Her tattoo was on the wall at the second fire, too.

Marine looked around the room and tried to see if anyone else was noticing a pattern, but she figured it didn't stand out at the second fire scene any more than it did at the first one. The tattoo was strategically placed amongst the graffiti on the wall. She tried to look at it carefully to make sure she wasn't forcing the shape to look like her tattoo. She hoped it didn't look like it. She knew it did, and she couldn't mention this second sighting. Not yet, not before she had a chance to talk with Chet. Damn, she wished Drake were here, now.

EIGHTEEN

....

STORM OF NAILS

The morning sun broke through the window curtain as Marine readied herself for her first full day off on her four-day break. As she went to sleep the night before, she listened to Lisa Marie Presley's album, *Storm of Nails*. The title song was still buzzing in her mind as she walked into the kitchen. The newscaster said on the radio, "And on the forecast for—" She came up short in her steps as she got a cold chill. Rubbing her arm, she wondered what kind of day she would have. She turned and began to prepare her coffee. Aunt Betsy walked in.

"Good morning," she said as she placed a basket in the sink. "I've been walking along the banks of the creek this morning and gathered greens for us to have with dinner. You will be here this evening, right?"

"Those are beautiful. And, yes, ma'am, I will. I thought I'd head over to the firehouse and visit with Shift B. They're working this morning, and then I may go check out Tony and Korena's Pampered Healing Day Spa. I saw that they are offering specials right now. I don't remember ever having a massage. Several times, I have looked at their shop window, as I have driven by. I figured today was the day for me. Then, I'm topping it off with a visit to that hairdresser friend of yours. What's her name?"

"You mean Peggy's Place?"

"Yes. I'm due for a new do. This shaggy head is starting to get on my nerves."

"It sounds like you have a very busy day planned. Will you be able to fit it all in?" Aunt Betsy winked at Marine. She then placed homemade cinnamon rolls fresh from the oven at the exact spot that gave Marine a perfect whiff. The sweet aroma of cinnamon made her mouth water.

"I'm thinking I should insert a visit to the gym, too. You're going to fatten me up yet. I feel like a pig getting ready for winter slaughter." They laughed.

The Fire of Revenge

"It will be good for the three of us to be together."

"Yes. I can't think of any other place I'd rather be."

Marine got up, put her plate and coffee mug in the sink, and then bent down and gave Aunt Betsy a kiss on her cheek. "See ya later."

"You have a good day."

As Marine walked out to the Jeep, she hoped that she wasn't right, but she had an uneasy feeling that a storm was brewing.

* * * * *

As she walked toward the firehouse from her parked Jeep, Marine couldn't help but stop and take a look around. "I am a firefighter," she said to no one in particular. She was developing a sense of pride in her work and she hoped that she'd live up to the expectations of her fellow firefighters. She patted her pocket that held her commemorative coin.

Walking into the firehouse kitchen, she could hear laughter and a familiar voice. It was Crab.

"Letsco, what are you doing here? It's your day off." Crab said as he got up out of his chair and walked over to her. He put his arm around her shoulder and introduced her to the members of B Shift. "We're talking about the new generation of kids, how easy they got it, and how corporal punishment is frowned upon now. Grab yourself some coffee and a seat."

Marine looked around and found all the guys staring at her. She wondered how she'd fit in. She could hear Fish's words, "Just listen." One of the guys continued with his story.

"Something happens to these kids today. They have no idea about what it takes to wait and why sometimes life is painful," the Lieutenant for the shift said as he got up to refill his coffee cup.

"Don't I know it, Frank." Crab chimed in. "I used to have a Pops who was on the fire department in upstate. He worked twenty-four on and twenty-four off. I hated it when I got into trouble and Ma would say, 'You wait till your Pop gets home.'"

Marine could tell that Crab was, as usual, his cynical self. Fish had told her that he always looked at life with a negative view. He continued.

"I was ten and my brother, Henry, was eight. We had gotten Red Ryder B-B guns for Christmas. I believe it was '80. Me and my brother had just finished watching the *Battle of the Bulge* on TV. Our favorite part was the 'Siege of Bastogne.' We lived in a house that was on a tenant farm. This was Pop's second job. On the farm were several prized bulls. Now, mind you, these were large beasts.

"Henry and I decided we would be members of the One-Hundred and First Airborne, and so, we advanced to a forward position at a rail fence. Sighting the enemy, we began to fire. If you've ever seen the nut sack of a 3,000-pound bull, you'd realize it was an easy target for two boys taking Bastogne. It seemed like a good idea at the time. This massive bull turned into a roaring locomotive and ran through fences as though they were toothpicks. He ended up two fields away.

"If Pops was on, sometimes I'd have to wait a whole day and a half before I got my beating. That was the longest two days of my life—pure hell."

The guys busted out laughing. Marine enjoyed seeing this side of Crab and wondered how the other guys were when they let down their macho attitude. She also knew, from what she'd seen so far, making it in the fire department or even moving up in ranks without the support and respect of these guys would not happen. It was a tight knit group.

"Well, guys, this has been fun. I need to go do some things. You have a great day and stay safe." Marine got up, walked over to the sink, and started to wash her mug.

"Probie, what the hell are you doing?" Marine turned to Crab, "You don't wash the dishes unless you're on duty. Go on, get outa here." Marine smiled and let the mug slip into the dishwater.

As she walked back to her Jeep, she knew something had changed in her life. A new sense of belonging was coming over her since she donned her fire gear. During one of the many times that she and Fish talked, he had shared that something happens to a person when they become a firefighter. He shared how a need to care for his work and the people he works with developed in him. "It becomes a dedication," he had said.

Marine inserted her key, and then opened the door to the Jeep as she thought about her feelings. It was a surprise to her that she felt a need for service coupled with a profound sense of pride in her job. This feeling must be what enabled a person to enter a burning structure.

The Fire of Revenge

Pulling the door to her Jeep closed, she started up the engine. It roared alive, yet she could hear Fish telling her that the history of firefighting would one day boil up in her soul. She turned and backed out of the parking lot. She could feel that history wrapping around her. It made her smile.

* * * * *

Marine walked into Tony & Korena's Pampered Healing Day Spa, hoping it would be a glorious retreat from stress. She had overheard some of Aunt Betsy's friends at Belle's mention the new spa. It was located just a couple doors down from the restaurant on Main Street. The entrance opened up into a reception area that immediately set the mood for relaxation—low lighting, soft music, and comfortable chairs. To the right sat the receptionist.

"Hello, I'm Nancy. So glad you dropped in. May I help you with an appointment?"

"Hi, Nancy, I'm Marine. Actually, I was hoping you took walk-ins. I felt like I needed to try this today. I've never had one before. At least, I don't remember. I have about three hours available. How long does a massage last? Is it possible to fit in an appointment today?"

"Oh, well, let me look at the appointment book. Korena and Tony, the owners, are with a client now. You've not had a massage before?"

"No, not that I remember."

Nancy laughed. "Not that you remember. That's funny." She flipped through the appointment book. "We do have a special going on for those new to massage; it is called the Get to Know Us Massage. It takes about thirty minutes and costs fifty-five dollars. It looks like we could book you for one o'clock today. Will that work?"

I looked up at the clock; it was eleven thirty. "Book me. I'll be back. What should I wear?"

"You will keep your street clothes on. They will work with you and help you learn how to relax, which is what is important."

"Oh, how cool. Okay. I'm going to go get my hair done, so I'll be back at one."

"Great. See you then, Marine."

* * * * *

Peggy's Place was located off Main Street in the Old Stage Mall. Peggy, the owner, had operated a shop there for many years. Aunt

The Fire of Revenge

Betsy recommended her highly. Having not met Peggy before, Marine felt a little odd as she walked through the door. Her worries were laid to rest as Peggy greeted Marine with a warm smile.

Peggy looked up from her books. "Hello!"

"Oh, it's you. I had no idea when we met the other day at Peking that you were the same Peggy that Aunt Betsy spoke about."

"I didn't make the connection even though Aunt Betsy had called me today and she described you to a tee. But, I declare, I'm sort of dumb not realizing it was you. Since we really didn't get to speak directly with each other, let me introduce myself again. I'm Peggy Westbon. I must say, I won't be able to make you any prettier than you already are, but I'm sure I'll be able to help you have a new hairstyle you will enjoy wearing."

Marine offered her hand in greeting. Peggy's grip was sure but warm. "Glad to meet you again, Peggy. Aunt Betsy described you to a tee, too. It's funny. I wasn't looking for you in the restaurant. You're just as friendly and lovely as she said you'd be."

Marine took off her coat and hung it on the coat stand near the door. Peggy's shop had a large open curved window that showed the street in front and let in lots of morning light.

"I'm not sure I can do magic, but I'll try." They both laughed. "Come on in here and I'll see what we can do." Marine walked into the next room that held a sink with chair, two hair-drying units, and a styling counter with chair. "Come sit here at the sink and I'll give you a shampoo."

As Marine sat in the chair, she looked around the room. There were mirrors strategically placed on the south wall that gave the illusion the room was twice as large. It was a clever effect. When the cape was draped and tied around her neck, Marine sprang up in a panic. She had a flashback of knocking out a hairdresser before she realized what she was doing.

"Oh, can you not make that so tight?" Marine pulled at the cape around her neck. "I don't like it so tight around my neck."

"Sure, Marine." Peggy loosened it and asked, "Is that better?"

"Yes." Marine settled back and Peggy started the water to flow. When it was the right temperature, she began to wet Marine's head. The warm water flowing over her head was soothing. "Ah, that's what I needed," Marine said as she immediately began to relax.

Peggy's hands started washing Marine's scalp, massaging as she went. It felt wonderful. Just as Peggy finished, the door to her shop opened.

"Well, hello there. I haven't seen you for a couple of weeks." Peggy left Marine with her head back. From the angle, she couldn't see the person's face, but it sounded like a voice she recognized. Was it Drake?

Peggy said, "Well, sure. You can wait. I'll be finished here in about twenty minutes, or you can go next door to Flourz Café, get yourself some coffee and a pastry." Peggy wrapped a towel around Marine's head and sat her up, as the shop door closed. Looking out the front window, she saw Drake walk past.

"Do you know that gentleman?"

"I just met him a couple of weeks ago. He has been in here for one haircut. He must have liked my work."

"Do you do many men's hair?"

"I have a fair number. But, as you can imagine, I mostly do women."

"I guess you have a set of regulars?"

"Yes, but as they age, I begin to lose them, and then I have openings. I was glad Aunt Betsy suggested to you to give me a try. Now, what can we do for you today?"

"I think you should do what you think is best. I want a cut that is easy to manage. I'm a new rookie at the firehouse, as you know. I want my hair to be a little easier to care for. Yet, I want to still look like a woman."

Peggy moved her fingers through my hair. "You know—" she trailed off as her phone rang. "Give me a minute. Hello, Peggy's Place, this is Peggy. May I help you?"

Marine listened as Peggy responded to the voice on the other end.

"I think you know I will do what I can to help you. I know what you said to me yesterday. Yes, I will." Peggy hung up. "I tell you what. Have you ever dealt with someone who can't seem to trust anyone?"

"Yes. I have."

Peggy began to trim Marine's hair. "This lady came in here the other day asking if she could have the hair clippings off my floor. I told her sure. Then, she said the oddest thing. She asked me to bag up each one individually. Can you imagine? Look at that pile over there. Does she really think I'll take the time to separate out all that hair? The lady is crazy if you ask me."

"That is odd." A cold chill went over Marine, but she didn't know why. She had learned from working with Chet to pay attention to those warnings. As soon as her massage was over, she would go find Chet and talk with him. There was something about the idea of collecting human hair that bothered her.

Peggy continued trimming Marine's hair. "So, tell me about your wedding plans to that handsome firefighter. What is his name, again?" Marine asked as she watched Peggy work.

"Jerry Cline."

"And, where is he stationed?"

"He's a firefighter with Salem Station One. You know, I don't think I need to do much to your hair. I've got it shaping up nice. What do you think?"

"It's looking good. I haven't had it this short in a while. By leaving it shoulder length, I can still pull it back if I want. Back to you and Jerry. I had forgotten what he said about where he works. And, your wedding plans?"

"It's going to be a small wedding. We'll have a few friends, and then we'll head to the coast for a short honeymoon."

"Sounds lovely."

"So, do you want me to style it for you? It will take another five minutes or so to blow dry. Your hair is so thin, it will dry fast." Marine nodded.

While Peggy dried her hair, Marine thought about Peggy and Jerry getting married, starting a life. She wondered if she would ever have that kind of life. She watched Peggy work and decided that she would like to get to know her better.

Peggy held up a mirror so that Marine could see the back of her new cut.

"Oh, I love it," Marine said. "You really can work magic. How will I ever be able to replicate it? I had no idea my hair would curl like that."

"Here, you'll want this curling gel. It will help your natural curly hair to hold its curl longer and withstand the abuse of a fire helmet. Your hair curls much easier when it is short. Even though your hair is thin, it is heavy when it is long so it would pull your natural curl out. Would you like some hair spray?"

Marine nodded. "This really looks great."

The Fire of Revenge

They walked into the outer office. Marine stood at the counter as she got her money.

Peggy said, "Are you seeing Drake?"

Marine paid her. "No. I'm not."

"He sure looks hot. I think you should. I don't know much about him, but I bet he'd be fun."

"Why do you think that?" Marine wasn't sure what she wanted. Drake was intriguing, though.

"Oh, the sparkle in his eyes. He looks like someone that could have fun. And, he looks like he is looking for someone." Marine finished putting her change in her wallet. "How about we set your next appointment? When would you like to come back?"

"Hmmm. I don't know. What do you think?"

"Let's try six weeks first. Then, we can adjust up or down. That will give me a chance to see how fast your hair grows."

"Marine! Fancy seeing you here," Drake said as he walked through the shop door.

"Good to see you, too. When you're done, would you like to have lunch?"

"Sure. How long will we be, Peggy?"

"Oh, about fifteen minutes." Peggy winked at Marine.

"That works fine, Drake. I have an appointment at one. It's a little before noon. How about I meet you next door at Flourz and we get a sandwich?" Marine mouthed the words to Peggy that she'd see her in six weeks.

"Sure. See you then."

NINETEEN

....

TROUBLE

Sitting in Flourz, Marine looked at the clock. Drake was running behind. With only forty minutes to have lunch, she walked over to the counter and ordered two Italian subs with homemade chips and cold tea.

Drake came in the door.

"Sorry, I'm late. Peggy had to gather up your hair."

"Glad you mentioned that." They walked over to a table and took their seats to wait for the sandwiches. "Doesn't that concern you?"

"What? That she cleans up?"

"No, silly. That a strange woman called and asked her for hair clippings and to bag them separately?"

"Hmmm. Since you mention that, maybe. Why do you ask?"

"I know I'm supposed to know something about the gathering of hair clippings. And, I know it's not good."

"Have you told Chet?"

"Not yet. I just found this out. I'm not sure what I should say."

"You need to tell him everything. Chet is your doctor. He will be able to help you determine what a memory flashback is or if you are mixing up your life, and worrying for no reason. You should trust him."

"How is that possible? I don't even know what is real or not. How could *he*?"

"He'll be able to guide you to help you determine what is real."

"Drake, sometimes I think you say things like that to pacify me. You know something about my past life. Why won't you tell me?"

"Marine, it is not my place to tell you things you need to recall. I don't need to add to your burden."

"Number 34," the lady behind the counter said.

Marine got up to get the sandwiches. Drake grabbed the drinks. They sat down and began to eat. Marine realized she was hungry. She was also angry. Eating without talking was giving her the chance to let her temper calm down. She didn't want to confront him in the sandwich shop. While she ate, she wondered how she could learn what he knew. She was determined not to let her questions be put away so easily.

After finishing her sandwich, she got up, took her trash to the trash can, and refilled her tea. When she turned to walk back to the table, Drake had left; he had even left his trash. That SOB. She looked out the window only to find he was nowhere in sight. Turning back to pick up her bag, she wondered where he had gone in such a hurry and without saying a word.

* * * * *

As Marine walked into the spa, Nancy greeted her.

"Hello, Marine. Korena and Tony will be right with you. Please have a seat in one of the plush chairs. May I get you something to drink?"

"Thank you, but no. I just had lunch. That won't make a difference for me having a massage, will it?"

"Oh, no. You'll be fine. I hope you find that the massage will relax you."

Marine sat down and positioned her purse beside the chair. She hoped that Nancy was right. She thought back over her lunch with Drake. The stress building after Drake had left suddenly was going to bust her chest. She would welcome a chance to relax. She couldn't believe what a royal pain Drake was becoming.

"Hello, Marine. I'm Korena and this is Tony."

A striking, petite woman with long blonde, curly hair that flowed down below her shoulders greeted Marine with a warm smile. Tony was tall, with gray highlights in his hair that made him look chic, yet debonair. His handshake was firm and sure. Korena's palm was held tilted slightly from vertical; her grip was firm. Marine somehow knew this woman would help her relax. After the preliminaries and Korena's warm welcome, Marine started to do just that.

"You know, you both have been so welcoming. I think I'd like to try a regular massage. Is that possible?"

"Sure," Tony said. "We will leave the fee at the rate we quoted. We won't do a long massage since this is your first, but we will do what we think will help you get a good feel for what a longer massage would do for you."

"Yes." Korena nodded. "In that case, let me turn on the heat for the bed. When you undress, you can leave on your underwear if you feel more comfortable. Then, you want to get on the bed face down."

Tony flicked a switch on a lamp near the table. "I'll give you a few minutes, and then I'll knock softly to let you know I'm coming in."

"Thank you."

Korena and Tony allowed Marine to change out of her clothes, and then Tony came into the room. Marine was determined to enjoy the experience. Yet, she couldn't shake an uneasy feeling.

Tony adjusted the lighting and said in a soft voice, "Would you like more heat on the bed? We have a heated blanket under you and I can adjust the temperature if you like."

"No, I'm fine."

"First, I'll massage your back to help work the tension out of your upper shoulders. Then, I'll move to your arms and legs. Is that okay?"

"Yes. You work your magic, Tony. I'll lay here with the idea of relaxing."

"I'll do my best."

He moved the blanket down off Marine's shoulders and touched her back softly. It gave her reassurance.

"I'm placing warm oil on my hands. Are you comfortable?"

"Yes. It is nice to just lie here."

Tony began to massage Marine's back and it didn't take long for her to begin to relax in such a way she didn't remember feeling before. Time drifted by and she had no idea how long she had been lying there.

Tony spoke in a hushed tone, "I'm going to move down to your legs. I'll do one at a time. How are you feeling?"

"Like heaven. I should have done this a long time ago."

He removed the blanket on her right leg. He began to massage it and just as he touched where her tattoo was located, she felt a surge of energy crash in.

"No. Please stop!" She sat up and grabbed the blanket up around her neck.

"Marine? What's wrong?"

"I don't know. We have to stop. Now."

Tony walked out and closed the door.

Marine quickly dressed.

The Fire of Revenge

The panic was trying to rise in her throat, but she kept trying to calm down.

She walked out to the reception area where she paid Nancy.

"Please tell Korena and Tony that I am sorry, but I'll have to come back if they would allow me. It's not Tony's fault. I had a panic attack."

Marine put on her coat and went out the door.

* * * * *

It was twenty minutes before Marine pulled into Aunt Betsy's driveway. She went immediately back to Chet's office.

"Marine. Hello!" Marine almost ran into Aunt Betsy as she was closing the door to Chet's lab. "What's your hurry, dear?"

"I've got to see Chet. Is he busy?"

"He's not here."

"Oh God, really?"

"He should be back in about an hour. He had to go meet someone. What's happened?"

"Ah, well. It's kind of hard to explain."

"You can tell me anything; you should know that by now."

They walked back to the house and Aunt Betsy put on the teapot. "Would you like some

Jasmine Monkey Tea and a slice of apple tart? It just came out of the oven."

Marine could smell the cinnamon and apple wafting through the kitchen. "Yes, that would be nice."

"You sit down here and tell me from the beginning what's got you upset. Nothing is so bad we can't work things out together. Just like those firemen help each other, you and I can be our own support group."

Aunt Betsy set a cup before Marine with a tea bag. The hum of the water starting to heat filled her with a different sense. She thought about what Crab had said earlier about learning to rely on those who cared about her and what Fish had told her, too.

"Aunt Betsy, this may sound crazy."

"Trust me, dear. Nothing sounds crazy once you reach my age."

"I think I'm seeing ghosts and my memory might be coming back. I find myself seeing things that aren't there and thinking things that are real or might not be. Worse, I'm afraid I may hurt someone."

"Why do you think you will hurt someone?"

"I don't know. But, I know I *could* if I chose to."

"Marine, any animal can hurt others when it wants to. It's when we choose not to because we don't have to that makes us human."

"I get that, Aunt Betsy. That's what scares me. There are times that the anger in me builds; I can feel my anger begin to overtake me. I know I can lash out and hurt someone. I can kill. I worry that the person I was before Chet met me is coming back. I'm scared of who I was then. When I have the flashbacks, I see death."

"Do you have any idea where you are?"

"I'm in different places. Once, I was on a ship. Chet never said anything about people dying on the ship, so I'm not sure if it was the cruise I was on or a different ship. And now, I keep catching glimpses of a lady that was on the cruise, Ana-Geliza. She was my cabin steward. But that can't be."

"Why not?"

"The last night on the ship, Ana-Geliza came to my cabin. We got into a fight; she was trying to kill me. I managed to get away from her. During the shuffle, she went over the railing and landed on a lifeboat below. I thought I killed her."

"Really?"

"Yes. But Drake said he took her to the infirmary. A fall like that, she should have died, don't you think?"

"Didn't you tell anyone?"

"No. Not even Chet. Only Drake knows. And now I have seen her three or four times."

"Seen who?" Chet said as he walked into the kitchen."

"Hi, Chet," Aunt Betsy said. She got up and went over to the stove. "Would you like some hot tea with a slice of apple tart?"

"Sure. What were the two of you talking about? Who have you seen, Marine?"

"Chet, I would have told you before, but Drake told me to keep it close until he was able to learn more."

"Tell me what?"

"Ana-Geliza."

"What?"

"I told you I thought I'd seen her in town. Well, now I think she is stalking me."

Chet looked at Marine, and then began to rub his forehead in a slow, determined manner "Is there more?"

"Yes. I saw the pattern of my tattoo, again, at the second fire."

"Where?"

The Fire of Revenge

"On a wall again. But, this time I saw it in a photograph of the fire scene."

Chet looked worried, but he didn't say much for a minute or two. Marine started to speak again, but Aunt Betsy motioned her to wait. Chet then said, "What you are telling me warrants more study into what your tattoo means and why you seem to keep running into the symbol. You have a lot going on with your new job. Do not worry about it. Let me do some research. You focus on your firefighting, doing the best you can. That is what is important right now." Chet got up and went out of the room.

Marine looked at Aunt Betsy and she shrugged her shoulders. She then wondered if she was making more out of the tattoo than she needed to. After all, nothing came out of the research Chet did on the tattoo before.

"Aunt Betsy?"

"Yes."

"I'm going to head upstairs. Thank you for the delicious tart and tea. I have some thinking to do."

"Marine, take yourself a nice long, warm soak. You'll feel so much better."

Marine walked over to the sink, placed her dishes down, and gave her a hug. "Thanks, Aunt Betsy."

* * * * *

"When I left earlier, I told Marine that I would do more research," Chet said as he walked into the parlor where Aunt Betsy sat crocheting. "How did she react when I left?"

"You could say that she was perplexed. She went upstairs to think. What's going on, Chet?"

"How much did she tell you?"

"She told me about her cabin steward. What is her name?"

"Ana-Geliza." Chet moved to a nearby chair.

"Yes. And then you came into the room."

"Did she say anything else before I came in?"

"She was very upset when she arrived home. I told her you were out. That seemed to cause her to get more nervous. She was beginning to tell me more when you came in."

Chet walked over to the fireplace. He took the fire iron from the tool set and poked at the fire. "We've got to keep Marine's mind off these events and keep it focused on her job. Will you help me?"

The Fire of Revenge

"Yes, Chet. I will help you, but to what end?"

"It may mean the difference between her life and death."

TWENTY

....

STRONGER

The morning seemed to be flying by for Marine as she put the last load of washed clothes into the dryer. Once she finished the chores, she could spend the rest of the day looking for an apartment or maybe even a nice duplex. It would be good to have a place she could call her own. Something she vaguely remembered having before. She wondered where she had lived before. The last eight months, she'd barely thought about what her life before might have been like. Now that she was starting a new life, she wondered if she should start thinking about it or just let it be.

Marine walked into the kitchen and placed her coffee mug on the counter. "Hello?" She looked outside to see if Aunt Betsy was in the back and noticed that Chet's car wasn't in the driveway. He must not have arrived yet, she thought.

She went back to the counter and poured some more coffee into her mug, added some sweetener, and a touch of cream. She stood there swirling the coffee as she began to think about what kind of place she'd like to have. She turned and saw Aunt Betsy standing in the doorway.

"You were in deep thought," Aunt Betsy said as she walked over to her. "You didn't hear me come in."

"No. I didn't. You actually startled me a little. I must be finally relaxing."

Aunt Betsy placed another fresh basket of greens into the sink. "I was out in the garden seeing what greens I could gather before our next snow. I can't seem to get enough of them in the winter. I love fresh greens cooked in bacon fat with a good size slice of cornbread and homemade apple butter. What are you planning to do today?"

"I was thinking about going out and looking for a new place to move into. I'm not sure what kind of place I want, though."

"You should go look at many different places. That way, you'll find one that suits you."

"Yes, but I don't know that I have any idea what suits me. I do like it here."

"So, why move?"

"Oh, I don't know. I feel funny coming into your home each night."

"Is it because of the fact you sleep across the hall from me and feel you can't have a man friend over?"

"Aunt Betsy. You are a pistol." Marine smiled. "Well, yes. That is one thing."

"When are you planning to go looking?"

"I thought I'd head out in about an hour. Why? Would you like to go with me?"

"Yes. I think that would be nice. I'll be ready."

* * * * *

"Well, the last two we've looked at just haven't done it for me. What's next on the list?"

Aunt Betsy flipped the newspaper over and pointed to the next circled apartment for rent. "This one is located just two blocks over. It borders the Jefferson Forest and has a main house in front of it. I think you might like that one. Let's go see it."

"Okay. Where did you say it was?"

"Take a left here and go for about two blocks, and then you should see the driveway."

"Aunt Betsy. This is heading right for Trout House Falls. What gives?"

"Pull up into the driveway all the way to the back and I'll show you."

After parking the car, Marine and Aunt Betsy got out of her Jeep.

"Come with me back here, to your new apartment. I've had Chet working all morning at moving out his lab and moving you in. I hope you like the furnishings I've selected for you." Aunt Betsy opened the door.

"Oh, Aunt Betsy." Marine walked around what had been Chet's office and was now her living room. A wall of windows offered a view of the west of the property that extended over to the falls and Trout Creek. Plush chairs and side tables set next to the windows with a small dining table behind. It offered a perfect spot to enjoy a meal, read, and relax. "I'm speechless. It is perfect."

"You haven't seen the rest. Come with me."

Aunt Betsy led her to see the kitchen with dinette area, and a quaint bathroom next to her bedroom. The bedroom was laid out with a Victorian style bed, dresser, and all of her things had been placed into the closet as well in the drawers.

"You and Chet have worked a miracle. I can't believe this. Where will his office be now?"

"We had talked about his need to move into town for some time. He has gotten himself a comfy little office off Main Street. It works so much better because he can come here for family visits and not feel like he is coming here only to work."

Marine walked around the living room again, taking it all in. She stopped at one of the chairs with her hand resting on its back. "I have never felt so loved before. Thank you. Thank you, both."

"Now, what do you plan to do with the rest of your day?"

Before Marine could answer, the phone rang. "Do you think it is for Chet?"

"No. I'm sure it would be for you. You better answer it."

"Hello? Yes. Okay, I understand."

"Who was it?"

"It was Captain Wayne. It appears I must come into work early. He said I'd be able to take my remaining two days off during the next pay period. I'm to report tonight at eight."

"Well, then, I will leave you to enjoy your time here getting acquainted with your new digs."

"Aunt Betsy, you sound so hip."

She laughed as she closed the door behind her.

Marine took off her coat and walked about her new place looking at the kitchen. She walked back into the living room and noticed the TV. She hadn't seen it before. They had thought of everything. She turned it on and began to surf channels. She found a show called *Castle*. She decided she might as well get in some television watching and relaxing before she had to go back to fighting fires.

Several hours went by. Marine had watched two television shows that were new to her. She decided to go visit Aunt Betsy and walked in the back door of the house.

"Hello?"

"Come on in!" Aunt Betsy was standing at her stove stirring something in a pot. "Are you all settled in?"

"You know I am. You and Chet didn't leave anything for me to do. I'm almost embarrassed to say I spent the last few hours watching TV."

"Did you learn anything?"

"Actually, I did. Can you take a break, have some tea, and let me tell you about it?"

"Sure. Put the water on and I'll get us some ginger snaps."

Aunt Betsy and Marine took their seats at the kitchen table.

"Now, while we wait for the water, tell me what you learned."

"It was almost serendipitous. I found this TV show called *Castle*. He, Castle, is a writer that shadows a woman police officer, Becket. Anyway, while watching a couple of episodes, I realized that I was enjoying trying to figure out the solution to the murder or crime along with them. Then, I watched this show called *Bones*. Again, I was intrigued by the story's central character, Dr. Brennan, who knows a lot about bones and the human skeleton. The investigations that the FBI special agent, Booth, and Dr. Brennan do together were entertaining."

"Okay. So you like two TV shows. And?"

The teapot whistled. Aunt Betsy got up, poured the hot water into the mugs, and replaced the pot on the stove.

"Well, I've been tinkering with the idea that I might like going into fire investigations.

Watching these shows helped me figure out that I think I would really like it."

"What triggered you to think you might like fire investigations in the first place?"

"I don't really know. Except, I have been very curious about some things I saw at the two fatal fires I've fought. I was intrigued when Fish took me through the sites and we studied the scene. I just think I'd like it and these shows helped me to decide to at least check into it."

"Sounds like you might have found a potential long term career path to follow. You should check it out. Do you know anything about what it takes to become a fire investigator?"

"No. But, I know just the guy to ask."

"Marine, can I say something to you?"

"Sure. You've done so much for me today already. Shoot."

"I have to laugh. I'd be careful how you use the word *shoot*." Marine smiled. "You seem to be growing stronger in that you are more confident. You are facing a new life. Today, you moved into a new apartment."

"Yes, all of twenty feet away from where I was living."

The Fire of Revenge

"True. But, you can come and go at your own leisure. And, you can have company without fear of interfering with my life. For that, I think you are doing very well. You know, my mother used to say to me all the time, what doesn't kill you makes you stronger. I think you are living proof of that."

Marine got up and wrapped her arms around Aunt Betsy. She kissed her cheek.

"You are a treasure. Thank you. Now, sadly, I must get ready to go to work. See you in the morning."

TWENTY-ONE

....

AS THE SKY FALLS

Walking into the firehouse, Marine reflected on her decision. She had decided when she woke up that she was not going to worry about her tattoo. She had also figured out that she couldn't have seen Ana-Geliza. Chet would have been worried if he thought she had. She was supposedly dead. Marine stopped walking and looked down at the ground. She was still trying to reason with herself.

"Are you okay?" Captain Wayne said as he walked up beside her.

"Yes, sir. I was thinking."

"Do your thinking inside, FNG. We've got a shift to get started. Thanks for coming in to cover for Doc. He has gotten the flu."

"Yes, sir. No problem."

Wayne walked on in front of her. Marine had started to accept the fact any chance they had for a relationship was gone now that she was working under his supervision. She walked over to her locker and checked her gear. Laughter came rushing out of the kitchen. She went in to see what was going on. All the guys from Shift C, her shift, were sitting around the table.

"Hello everyone," Marine said as she took a seat next to Fish.

"Hello, FNG." Crab smiled. "We're sharing war stories." She looked at Fish.

"No, not real war stories. But, that's how we sometimes refer to it when we've fought hard fires. And, we're talking about our partners who often helped to save us."

Marine thought, he must have read her mind. She looked around the room and could see solemn looks on the guys' faces. "So, what happened to the laughter I heard earlier? You guys look too sad."

Crab patted Marine on the back as he handed her a cup of coffee. "You'll get used to our mood swings. It is what happens when we remember those who've fallen. We share the

The Fire of Revenge

fun times, we laugh, and then we fall silent as we think about them being gone."

Fish spoke up, "You've got to have faith not only in the religion you believe, but in each other. That will pull you through the hard times when fighting hard fires. When I first became a firefighter, we had very little training—they gave me my gear, told me that I was going on calls. When I got on the truck for my first fire, the Captain told me to get with this other firefighter named Dennis. He said that we were to be partners. For years, I looked up to Dennis as my guiding light. We were the A team—first in, last out. We seemed to always find ourselves in tight spots. I respected what we did together.

"It was about twenty years later, Dennis had retired, and we met for lunch one day. Dennis shared that he appreciated how I had helped him learn to be a firefighter and helped to get him through those tight spots we had found ourselves in. I asked Dennis what he was talking about.

> *"Dennis said, 'You taught me everything I needed to know and survive in those fire situations.'*

I said, 'Dennis, when we met that was my first fire ever.'

Dennis said, 'What? That was only my second. I thought you were the experienced firefighter that had come from another station.'

I said, 'No, partner, you were the experienced firefighter!'

We had a sobering moment when we realized we were both Probies together."

Fish looked at Marine.

"You've got to learn to trust your instincts, your gut feelings, as that is what will help you when you most need it. And, because you're part of a team, it takes the team to survive. Your partner is the most important person in your life when you're in a fire."

Marine looked at him and nodded her understanding. "Were you ever scared?"

Crab stood up, "Anybody that says they are not scared, he's not a liar, he's a *damn* liar. I'll go one further. You know that you should be scared. Hell, it's natural. But, FNG, it's what keeps you alive." He walked over to the coffee pot. "Anybody need a refill?" Several held up their mugs and Crab went around the table filling their cups.

The Fire of Revenge

Marine took a sip of her coffee, "Aren't *all* fires bad?"

"Yes and no," LT chimed in. "We sometimes call a fire a *good* fire or *good job*. But, we don't mean to say it is good in the sense of being well behaved or effective. What we mean is that we did a good job fighting a tough fire. Yet, we probably also got our butts kicked. We're worn out after fighting a hard fight."

As Marine listened, she realized that she was observing the fire department's culture—their philosophy of life and death. She was beginning to understand why this group was such a tight-knit group, and as such, why it was hard to become a part of it.

"Well, boys, I got one for you," Roy said as he reached for a sausage ball. "Sorry, let me eat this. I happen to love these things. Thanks, Crab, for making them." Everyone nodded in agreement.

Roy continued with his story after he took a long gulp of coffee. "I was working at Station Seven, years ago. Me and Firefighter Salvio, we were partners then. We were with Sergeant Decker. We were doing a search of an apartment house that was on fire. It was thick white smoke, so we were crawling around the rooms searching for anyone trapped. Salvio and I went right and the Sergeant went left. In a short while, we heard Sergeant Decker screaming he was trapped and he couldn't move; something had him."

Roy stopped, got a drink of coffee, and then said, "We crawled around the wall and found Sergeant Decker pinned to the floor by a large, cast iron sink. The anchor bolts had burned away due to the fire that was on the other side of the wall. The copper and lead plumbing pipes were still attached and had wrapped around the Sarge's air bottle with the sink resting on his back. He couldn't roll over, he couldn't crawl, and he couldn't stand up. He was stuck. Me and Salvio rolled over on our backs laughing our asses off. It was the funniest damn thing we ever saw. Sarge called us assholes and demanded we get him free. Finally, we picked the sink up and got him free. We finished searching the floor we were on. As we're going down the stairs, Sergeant Decker threatened our lives if we told anyone. We promised we wouldn't tell *anyone*. We told the entire department. Sergeant Decker is now a Chief in another city. However, I wouldn't mention this story to him if you ever see him."

The Fire of Revenge

Everyone had a hardy laugh.

"Marine," Roy said, "don't get me wrong. It's good to laugh. But, fire has a serious side. People die. Sometimes *our* people."

"Have any of you come close?"

"Yes. Several of us," Captain Wayne walked in and sat at the table with us. "In the eighties and nineties, when we had an unusually large number of arson fires, firefighting became a war. We lost many of our brothers. In one bad fire, we lost an entire shift of eight men and in another we lost an entire company of twenty-four."

"Captain, I'd like to share about one of those. I was there." Cotton Top spoke up. "The fire department has been good to me, but that doesn't mean I haven't had my moments. Mr. John Walker became my best friend after the bad one.

"My partner and my Captain died in a warehouse fire that was later found to have been one of those set by an arsonist." Cotton Top paused and gathered his thoughts. "We went in. We thought people were trapped. The firefighting had been going on for a while. No one realized that a lot of water had collected in one of the upper floors. The weight brought the above floors down on them. I managed to get out of the way because I hadn't made it all the way in. The rubble crushed them. They didn't have a chance. The newspaper tried to imply that we shouldn't have gone in, but we had to."

Cotton Top stopped, and then said, "It took me a long time not to think I was supposed to have died with them. At the funeral, many of our brothers came to show their support. It still brings tears to my eyes. It's been several years now."

"All of these stories are important for you to hear as the newest member, but one thing you've got to remember. You've got to be able to get the job done. The public is counting on you. They expect you to save their property, to save their lives—so, you need to perform." Fish placed his cup in the sink and pointed to Marine. "You're with me today."

"On the subject of performing, how about let's perform our equipment checks?" Captain Wayne said as they all got up and started to work.

* * * * *

The Fire of Revenge

"Battalion Two. Stations Three and Seven – Respond to Second Alarm Assignment to an industrial fire – Massey Storage Facility on Madison Avenue – 22:30," the speakers hummed.

"This ride is ten minutes out," Fish said. "As a second alarm, it means our station was called as a second company to help fight the fire. Each alarm doubles the resources of what is being used. There will be a truck and an engine already operating at the scene from the first alarm. So, when we arrive, we will double the size of the resources, which means there will be two engines and two trucks. If there is no progress made, then the Incident Commander or IC will call for a third alarm, which will double the force to four engines and four trucks. And so on. Every fifteen minutes, the IC will determine if another alarm is to be called. You stay close to me. I want you to put into practice your reading smoke skills. You were taught what to look for at The Academy, Now, when we get closer; I want you to tell me what you can tell about the fire from the smoke you see."

Before the engine had reached the scene, the IC came over the truck radio calling for a third alarm.

Fish leaned over to Marine. "Get ready to go straight to work when we stop. It's already a bad one."

The ride was quiet to the scene. Everyone knew this was going to be a long night.

As they got closer, Marine began looking for the scene. She thought she could see a glow above the city lights in the sky, but she wasn't sure. Then, when they pulled down the street, she could see the lights from the two aerial trucks where firefighters were applying water to what looked like it could be a six-story building.

Marine leaned over to where the guys were pointing. "There is a big, dark black plume of smoke coming up, FNG. You know what that means?" Fish said as he reached for his helmet.

"Yes. The fire might be a bad one."

"You could say that. We are the second alarm. And, from the black plume, we know the hydrocarbons are burning, which means something nasty is going on. The first alarm has been here a while. We don't see any white smoke, which means they haven't found the heart of the fire yet. Come on boys, it's time to go to work," LT said as the pumper came to a stop.

The reflective scotch light on the jackets and pants of the firefighters showed that they were moving around in chaos yet were organized—much like a beehive appears when you observe them foraging during the honey flow. Marine marveled at the comparison she had just made despite the fact that she had no idea how she knew how beehives worked. Marine turned back and watched the firefighters, as the engine pulled into place. Each firefighter knew what to do. Some were working on the roof to ventilate while others were entering the warehouse at different points to attack the fire at its source.

LT picked up the mic and said, "Engine twenty-seven on scene." The mic clicked off.

The radios were flipped over to the external speakers of the trucks and engines. Instructions were blaring out all around.

"Engine twenty-seven, IC wants you down on the D side to do entry." the voice directed.

Fish leaned forward and said, "The IC just told us that we have to move to the right side of the building, the 'D' side, to see what is happening. LT will give us directions from there. Again, you stay with me."

Marine nodded.

Sergeant Roy maneuvered the engine to drive to the right side of the building. The police, in their haste, had left their cars blocking the street. Roy, an expert fire engineer, used the bumper of the engine to nudge the first police car into a second one. Then, he pushed them enough that it opened a path where he could then drive through.

"That's why fire trucks and engines have big bumpers," Fish smiled.

The engine came to a stop, and all began to unload. An upset police officer walked up to LT. It was obvious that he was mad as hell about his police cars.

LT just stared at him. Then, he turned to us and continued, "Crab, Willie, and Cotton-Top. You men go in and assess what's happening. Fish and Probie, you stay here and be grunts if I need ya."

Watching them go in, the idea of getting to see the fire from the inside came over her. She felt dizzy. Suddenly, she could smell burnt flesh. "Fish, do you smell that?"

"No. Probie. What do you smell?"

The Fire of Revenge

"Burnt flesh."

"How do you know what burnt flesh smells like?"

"I don't know." And then, just as clear as though she was watching a television screen, she saw the bodies lying on the ground. She looked at Fish, but it wasn't Fish, it was her friend. She was remembering the fire at the nightclub. It was all coming back. She moved away from Fish and opened up the engine side door. Inside was a bottle of water. She opened it and poured it on her face.

"Are you okay?" Fish walked up. "Probie. I've been calling you. Are you okay?"

"Yes. I got real hot. I needed water."

"It is getting hot."

LT walked up to us. "I need you two to take air bottles and hose up to three. Crab and his team will know to look for them at the stairwell. Probie, can you handle it?"

"Yes, sir." Fish looked at me and I gave him a look of confidence—to trust me.

"Because there's no smoke here, we won't put on our air packs. We can carry more equipment and move quicker up the stairs and get back down." Fish began handing me the bottles and he grabbed the hose. "When you're ready, we'll go up those stairs, deposit the stuff, and get back down. You got me?"

"Yes, sir."

Fish was making the turn at the second floor top landing as Marine came up behind him. A door slammed as she made it to the second floor. Marine saw somebody behind Fish. Then, he started to go down. Dropping the bottles, she ran to him.

Grabbing the person from behind at the collar to deliver a foot strike to clip him in the back of the knees, Marine fell short. He outmaneuvered her. Her fingers gripped his collar tighter.

While she wrangled the person around, Marine realized it was a female. She saw the face. It was Ana-Geliza.

Ana-Geliza's anger seemed to soar as her eyes glowed with insanity. Pausing was a mistake when Ana-Geliza hit Marine's shoulder just about dislocating it. Staggering back, the two got into a hand-to-hand street fight—knocking and hitting, trying to take each other out. Falling through the doorway into the open area of the warehouse of the second floor, they hit the floor with a loud thud.

The Fire of Revenge

Ana-Geliza said, "You know you're going to die."

Twisting out of Ana-Geliza's grip, Marine made a dash deeper into the warehouse. A pipe came whizzing past Marine. Instantly, Marine picked it up and ran toward her, using the pipe as a baton. The fight turned into one of life or death. From deep inside her, the moves she needed to do came rushing back—each movement came without a second thought.

The turnout gear gave her protection, but it also was hampering her mobility and the ability to fight back effectively. As Marine swung, Ana-Geliza grabbed her arm. Marine was not as fast as she needed to be. Ana-Geliza managed to knock her to the ground. The pain seared up through her shoulder and down her spine.

While grappling on the ground, Marine flipped Ana-Geliza over and got on top. In as swift a motion, as she could manage with the fire coat on, she slid to the side and grabbed Ana-Geliza's arm while putting a foot on her face. Marine pulled back with everything she had on her elbow.

"Aaaggh. I'll kill you, bitch!"

"You're going to have to do more than you're doing now to do that," Marine yelled as she slammed her fist into Ana-Geliza's face.

Ana-Geliza appeared to be knocked out. Marine got up and started to walk over to Fish to see if he was okay. Ana-Geliza grabbed Marine's shoulders and tried to use her leg to take Marine down. But Marine managed to grab her opponent in a wristlock, and she turned as Marine heard a shoulder snap. Ana-Geliza staggered back but stayed on her feet.

Marine turned to go help Fish. Ana-Geliza came up behind her again. Marine turned just as the pipe came down beside her head, hitting her shoulder. She staggered. The turnout gear was saving her. But, if she was going to help Fish, she would have to take Ana-Geliza out once and for all.

The fight resumed. The two scuffled and knocked each other's legs out from under each other. They moved around the room grabbing whatever they could find to use as a weapon. All the while, the fire seemed to be moving closer. It was getting hotter. Marine glanced and saw that smoke was moving into the room.

Ana-Geliza came at her. Marine fell on her back; moved her legs in close, and as she came

The Fire of Revenge

at her, Marine flipped Ana-Geliza over. She hit the gate of the freight elevator and crashed through it. Marine managed to crawl to the edge where she could see that Ana-Geliza was hanging on with one hand. She leaned over and grabbed her wrist.

She screamed, "You worked for TRANS just as I did. You were an assassin and killed my brother." As Ana-Geliza spoke, a flashback to the fire in the building where Ana-Geliza's brother died came into Marine's view. "You were the assassin that killed my brother. Your death is my payback. I'm taking you down with me."

Marine could see dark smoke starting to come up the elevator shaft. At the same time, she could feel her grip of Ana-Geliza's hand slipping. She tried to get her other hand down, but she couldn't reach her without her help.

"I can't hang on and grab you, too. Ana-Geliza, you've got to give me your other hand."

Marine's grip slipped.

Ana-Geliza slipped away and disappeared in the billowing smoke.

Marine pulled herself away. The second floor was covered in smoke. She managed to get on her feet and made a run to Fish. He was lying face down. Marine dragged him down the stairway, trying to protect his head, and got him out to the street.

"I need help!" she yelled.

LT came running over, looked at Fish and Marine, and then said, "What the hell happened to you two?" He clicked his mic on his coat and spoke, "This is Engine Twenty-Seven, D side. I need a medic unit with one firefighter down."

Fish began to cough and rose up hacking.

The medics came. Marine knew that Fish would now be safe. She sat down near the engine and took off her helmet. The wetness she had felt was not sweat.

"FNG, you need a medic, too," LT said. He turned and told the medics working on Fish. "You'll go to the hospital with Fish."

While the medics began assessing her injury, LT called on his mic to Crab and told him he and his team needed to come get the air bottles and hose they needed. They would be on their own.

The ride to the hospital was quiet. Fish was on oxygen and had his eyes closed. She sat on the side with her head bandaged; it was throbbing. The pain seemed to worsen as she

The Fire of Revenge

thought about watching Ana-Geliza fall to her death. Something snapped. She knew everything. She rubbed her temples. Ana-Geliza was right. She was a killer. She had just killed Ana-Geliza, too.

TWENTY-TWO

MY SILVER LINING

While waiting to be released from the hospital, Fish's radio came on with an announcement, "Deputy Chief McGee, we're leaving Station Five at the scene for salvage and overhaul. Releasing all other units back to station. Release fire ground frequency. 0600."

"By the time we get back to the firehouse, we won't have to wait long for the guys to come in. I like fighting fire this way." Fish chuckled as he signed his release form.

Once they returned to the firehouse from the hospital, Marine and Fish walked into the kitchen where she began to make coffee. It felt comfortable to be able to do something and have a sense of self-sufficiency. The vulnerability that had swept over her after regaining her memory had made her feel dazed. The last five hours were as though she had watched them through a movie screen. As she pushed the button to start the coffee brewing, Marine thought about Ana-Geliza. Her death was unavoidable. It was either Ana-Geliza or Marine. It easily could have been both of them.

She looked at Fish standing in one of the fire truck bays and realized how close he'd come to death. Poor soul, he had no clue. And, if Marine could help it, she'd never let him know how her past nearly caused his death. Now that she had her memory back, she needed to figure out what to do. She liked it here. But, she knew who she was.

Fish walked back into the kitchen. "Man, my bladder feels better. Can you believe it? I couldn't take a whiz at the hospital after fighting a fire. Don't they know we hold it? What are you doing?"

"I was standing here watching the coffee brew. You want anything to eat? I could rustle us something if you like?"

"Well, now FNG, it's not your job yet, you know. But, sure, we might as well see what you can do in the food department."

The Fire of Revenge

Digging around in the refrigerator, she found a pot of Roy's leftover chili from two days before. She decided to spruce it up a little with some fresh chopped green onions, tomatoes, and Sriracha sauce. While chopping up the onions and tomatoes, she thought about who she was before. She looked down at her hand. The knife felt like it had a life of its own. Her hand increased with speed as she cut up the onions.

"Whoa, FNG." Fish called to her. "What are you doing there?"

She looked down and saw that the onions were pulverized. "Oh, don't you like your onions mashed? They add lots more spice that way." Slipping them over into the pot, she placed it on the stove. She reached up into the cabinet and found some cayenne pepper and diced, dried garlic to add to the mix. She stirred the pot, and as she did, a picture of a witch came into her mind as an evil feeling came over her.

"Now that you have the food on, come over here and sit a minute. We need to talk." Marine grabbed the pot of coffee and two mugs.

"How do you take yours?" She began to fill each mug.

"I like it the way I take my women," Fish smiled.

"Really, now. How's that?"

"Cold and bitter." They laughed. Marine returned the pot to the coffeemaker and sat down.

"I know how you must be feeling. It could have gotten dangerous in there. But, really, we were not in harm's way." Fish stirred cream into his coffee. "The fire was far away. The smoke thing. Well, a lot of the older guys will tell you, we didn't use to wear air packs at all when we went into a fire. You feeling okay?"

"Yes, Fish. I'm fine."

"You seem different."

"What do you mean?"

"You seem, well, I don't know. You seem more confident. You sure worked those onions to a pulp. You don't appear innocent, anymore."

She laughed. "I guess I'm not."

"Did you see who jumped me?"

"I don't know."

"Go get two pads of paper and two pencils."

Marine came back with them and sat back down at the table.

"Did they teach you how to do incident reports at The Academy?"

"Yes. But, they said we might have to be instructed how to do them for our particular department.

"I'll help you with it."

"Thanks."

"First off, a good incident report will answer the six 'W's—who, what, when, where, why, and how."

"How?"

"It ends in a *w*. Now, you will start with your name, the date, time, shift, the time we left the station, and the time we arrived back. Then, you write your story of what happened. I'll write mine."

They both began to write.

Marine found herself worrying about what she should or should not include. Telling the truth about who she was or what she knew about Ana-Geliza would not work.

Marine wrote how she and Sergeant Fisher had gathered up the bottles and hose and began to make their way up to the third floor.

When we were almost on the second floor, someone grabbed Sergeant Fisher. I dropped the bottles and ran up to him. But whoever it was, I couldn't see. My thought was that it was a homeless person in the building who was frightened. When he saw me coming up the steps, he let go of Sergeant Fisher. He took off running. I got up to the Sergeant, saw the person running away and tried to find him. It was smoky; I couldn't see anything. I went back to Sergeant Fisher and helped him down to the engine.

As she read over what she had written, she considered the choice she had made. The opportunity for a new life here was important, but it would only work as long as she let the old life die. Telling the truth would destroy any chance she might have. The risk was not worth it, not now.

After twenty minutes, Fish said, "Let me see what you got." He took Marine's pad and sat quietly as he read. "This is a better report than any of the other guys ever do. We'll get this typed up and signed, and then give it to LT when he returns. We will have some other forms to fill out, also."

"Hey, anybody home?" Roy came walking in with the rest of the engine company following.

"Man, that was a rough one," Roy said as he got himself some coffee. "Oh good. Food. I'm starved."

The rest of shift came in. Everyone was talking at once, getting coffee, and filling their bowls with chili while asking how Fish and Marine were doing.

Crab was taking a bite of his chili, "Fish and FNG, they recovered a body at the bottom of the elevator shaft. It was severely burned. The arms and legs had been burned away, but it appeared to be a female."

Fish said, "I wonder if she was the one that jumped me?"

Drinking her coffee, Marine sat back in her seat. LT walked into the kitchen.

"FNG and Fish, I need you two in my office; you need to do an incident report."

"We've already written them." Fish handed the pads to him and followed him into his office. LT sat at his desk and read.

LT said, "Good job." He looked down at the reports, and then he looked up at Marine. "FNG, for this being your first incident report, I think you need to teach these other guys how to do one. Both of you get out of here."

LT walked out into the kitchen. The next shift was starting to arrive. "Everyone, it's time to go home. We'll have our debrief tomorrow at the shift change."

* * * * *

When Marine walked into the house, she stopped. She was about to go up to her room, gather her stuff, and leave. But, she realized, she had her own place in the back. Besides where would she go? What would she do? She needed to find Drake and talk to him about what he knew about TRANS and Ana-Geliza. A thousand questions were going through her mind.

"Marine. Good morning." Chet said as he walked up behind her.

It was as if she was looking at Chet for the first time. "Good morning."

"Did you have a hard shift?"

"Yes."

"Marine. I'm so glad you're home." Aunt Betsy walked up to her and gave her a hug. "We heard there was a bad fire. Did you fight it?"

"Yes. Aunt Betsy. I fought it. It was a hard shift." She turned to walk out the door to head to her apartment.

"Won't you come sit and have some breakfast?"

"No. I think I should go have a shower and try to relax. I may eat later."

Walking around back to her apartment, Marine could hear a dog barking in the

The Fire of Revenge

distance. It felt strange to have her memory back and not talk about it with Chet and Aunt Betsy. Next to the door, she paused. A bird perched in a nearby bush chirped. The sun was shining brightly. At least it's not raining. Shutting the door softly behind her after walking into the cottage, she was overcome with a slew of emotions. She walked to her bedroom and laid her things on the floor. Sitting down on the bed, she began to take off her boots. It felt good to release her feet from their confined space. The leather seemed extra heavy. How long would this fog hang over her? When she finished, she walked into the living room and looked out the window.

What the hell happens next?

* * * * *

The hot water flowing from the showerhead helped Marine begin to relax. It felt good being back. She had no idea how much she missed her history—a part of herself had been missing and she didn't even know it. She began to dry off. Yet, sadness came over her as she struggled with remembering what she had done. Living in New Brook, she had come to realize she liked life. She didn't want to lose the affection and love of Chet and Aunt Betsy. She didn't want to trade what she had received for what she had so desperately wanted to leave.

After putting on her sweat pants and drying her hair, Marine was putting on her face cream when she heard a soft knock.

Opening the door, Chet smiled.

"May I come in?"

"Yes."

Chet walked in and looked around the room. "This turned out to be a perfect little apartment for you."

"Yes. It has. Thank you for all you did to make it possible. You and Aunt Betsy did a fantastic job surprising me. I like it here a lot, already."

"I am sure you do. Can we talk?"

"Yes. I am tired. But, we do need to talk."

They moved over to the plush chairs near the window. Chet sat down and immediately reclined the chair back.

"I didn't know these reclined."

"They are nice. Let me get right to it. You are different. When we saw you in the foyer of the house, it was obvious that this last fire was different. If there is one thing I have learned in my life, it is that the power of resilience is in the ability to bounce back."

Marine smiled.

"This is the point in our relationship when I would ask you to lie on my couch and I would sit in my chair with my notepad and cross my legs."

"I think we're beyond that."

Marine studied his face and decided she needed to figure out what he already knew.

"I'm going to tell you things only a very few people in the world know. I worked for a company that goes by the name of TRANS. I was a paid agent of theirs. My assignments required me to go all over the world. Most of the jobs involved me working as a government contractor using a unique skill set that the average person would never dream of acquiring."

She stopped to see his reaction. Chet nodded for her to go on. He didn't appear to be as stunned by the news as anticipated.

"Everything I did while working, whether overseas or on my homeland as an operative, was illegal. Espionage was and still is illegal. There is no *license to kill* like you see in those famous movies. The reality was that as a

TRANS agent, I had no need to have a license to complete any of the jobs I was expected to do.

"I used many different identities. So many that I don't even remember the one that is my real name." Marine paused for effect. "You realize, I remember everything now."

"Memories can become the ghosts of our past if we let them."

Marine got up and walked over to the window. "You are not surprised?"

"Not really."

"Why?"

"Let me say, you are not the first person I have met that worked at such a profession."

"Who else?"

"I am bound by my professional oath not to reveal information. It is their story to tell just as this is your story to tell, not mine."

Marine smiled at him. She wondered when he first learned Drake was MI6. It seemed Chet knew how to keep a secret. He was proving to be an honorable doctor that would not betray her trust.

"I think it is going to help me if I tell you the truth as I know it now. As shocking as it may be, I now have this new life in New Brook, but I can't unring the bell on the things I've done. These things have been haunting me. I hate myself for what I was—for what I've done. My job was my duty, but my morals told me it was wrong. I can see all the things I've done and the people I've hurt. I can't shake this."

Chet asked, "Do you wish to be who you used to be?"

"I wish to be who I've become."

"There are things about me that a lot of people do not know. I can help you even more, now that I know who you really are and you need to know who I really am."

Marine nodded. All she could do was feel her heart beating harder. It seemed to be beating fast enough it could burst. She walked back to her chair and sat down.

"This may seem odd to you now, but it will get better. About two weeks after nine-eleven, I was called up to New York to work with the public safety employees as they were beginning to deal with the tragedy that surrounded them. Since then, I've been working with a group of veterans through the VA that have been diagnosed with PTSD. We've been using a new methodology that is used on what they are now calling the morally injured. This is generally brought on because of the psychological wounds of war, which I believe you are suffering from."

"I guess I have been in a kind of war of my own making. Hell, Chet, whom am I kidding? I'm damaged goods." Marine got up, walked over to the buffet sitting next to the dining room table. She slammed her fist into the mirror that hung above it.

"Take it easy, Marine. Are you hurt?"

She looked at her fist and felt no pain, yet blood began to flow. "That was reckless."

Chet got up and went out the door. Marine walked back to her bathroom and began running water over her hand. All she kept thinking was how awful she was to have killed so many people. How would the fire department allow her to stay on the job? She began to sob.

Chet walked back in with Aunt Betsy carrying her first aid kit.

"Oh my, Marine," she said as she took her hand. "Here, let me fix this for you." She moved her hand around and checked it over. "It doesn't look like you need stitches, but your knuckles will be sore."

"It's what I deserve."

The Fire of Revenge

"When you are morally injured, Marine, you have struggles with what you did for your job, just as any soldier would feel conflicted with his or her moral beliefs when he or she kills someone. Does it make sense that what you are feeling is not your fault?" Chet handed Aunt Betsy some gauze.

Marine looked at him and wanted to believe what he said, but she found herself getting angrier. "Chet, I'm not sure I can do this right now. I still have a lot to think through."

"We've fixed part of you, but in doing so another part is broken. We've still got work to do."

"It seems having no memory was the best place to be."

"And, maybe your body knew that," Aunt Betsy said, as she tapped the end of the bandage in place.

"How will I explain this at work tomorrow?" She held up her hand and turned it around to look at it. "You know how to bandage a wound, Aunt Betsy."

"You do not need to explain anything, Marine," Chet said as they walked back into the living room. "You need to believe that the best decision you can make right now is the choice to move forward and to not look back. You will go to work as you have already. You will continue to fight fires. You will make new friends. And then, in time, you will begin to heal. You have started a new life here, in New Brook. Aunt Betsy and I are here for you, too."

"That's right, Marine. We won't let you face this alone. You listen to Chet. He knows his stuff. You should know that already. And, one more thing, if there is anything I've learned it is that every cloud has a silver lining."

Marine looked at them and wondered how she was so blessed to have them both in her life.

TWENTY-THREE

COLD WASH

Getting to the firehouse was a little harder than usual. Aunt Betsy had said Marine's knuckles would be sore—her entire body was one big ache, she thought as she maneuvered the Jeep into the parking lot space.

"There you are," Fish said as he walked up. "You've got to get into the kitchen. We're about to have a cold wash."

"A what?"

"Cold wash. It's when we gather to discuss a Shit Worker, which stands for send help and it is a terrible all-hands fire requiring all workers to report. We will talk about the event and all will come out in the wash. It's referred to as a cold wash because we do it a few days after such a fire."

"Okay. I'll bite. Is there a hot wash?"

"Yes, there is. We do a hot wash right after the event, sometimes on site." Marine smiled. "You think I'm pulling your leg."

"Well, you've got to admit. Some of these names are a little funny." They walked into the kitchen. The room was full of all shifts that worked the fire.

"Do you believe me now, FNG?" Fish slapped her on the back and they took their seats.

Captain Wayne stood in front and began explaining how the cold wash would work.

"Battalion Chief Whisman is here to oversee the process. We begin the cold wash by announcing that this was a K fire—there was a death. The body was found after the fire was out. It was located in the elevator shaft over on the D side of the building."

Marine looked at Fish. He leaned over and whispered, "In the old days, we called them *crispy critters*." He turned back to the Captain. Marine wondered how much they knew about that particular critter.

The Captain went on explaining how some of the firefighters would be called to give a statement about what they did.

The Fire of Revenge

"For the most part," the Captain said, "we will discuss here and now the events as we were instructed to act. I'll ask each of the LTs to share their fire ground operations. Lieutenant Ron James, you go first."

As LT spoke, Marine's mind raced as she tried to think of what she would say if they called her for an interview. She thought about Ana-Geliza's last words. Then, Marine heard Chet's words encouraging her not to give up. Looking around the room, she wondered what she would do if she couldn't become a firefighter because of her past. Marine placed her face in her hands as she rested her elbows on the table and tried to relax. She had to get a hold of her nerves.

Lieutenant James and the other three lieutenants had finished their reports. Marine heard Fish talking.

"Hey there, FNG. The Captain just said for you to report for an interview."

Marine looked at him as she slowly got up out of her seat.

"Okay."

She walked into the interview room wondering what she would do. The Captain and the Battalion Chief were sitting on the far side of the table with their backs to the wall.

"Take a seat there, Letsco," Captain Wayne said as he pointed to a chair directly across from them. "We have your report and we both have read it."

Marine looked at him and considered whether she should mention Ana-Geliza.

Captain Wayne continued, "We understand you're a rookie." He held up her report. "This is a well written and detailed account of the events. We see in the report that someone assaulted Sergeant Fisher. You state that you couldn't tell who the person was or anything about them. Is that correct?"

"Yes, sir."

"Could this person have been a female?"

"I couldn't tell."

"You didn't see anyone else at the scene?"

"No."

"Thank you, Firefighter Letsco. That will be all." As she went out the door, the Battalion Chief said, "Good job, Letsco."

Marine walked out into the firehouse and music was playing. She started to think about how lucky she was, and how Aunt Betsy was right. A silver lining might be in her reach.

The Fire of Revenge

As she walked toward the kitchen, she realized that playing on the radio was First Aid Kit's song *My Silver Lining*. The words spoke to her. They reminded her to keep on keeping on. Yet, she found she felt horrible that she lied to the Battalion Chief and Wayne, no differently than she did when she lied while doing a job for TRANS. She heard a voice telling her that she was slipping back to her old bad habits. If she was going to be free of her past, she needed to break the shackles of her old ways. But, she needed the will to make something good come out of the bad.

Fish walked up to her. "How'd it go?" Marine turned and looked at him. "Are you okay?"

"Not really. I don't know if I'm going to be good for the fire department."

"What did they say to you in there that caused you to think that?"

"Nothing really. I'm questioning my abilities to be a good firefighter."

"The fact you're questioning yourself means you've got the right stuff to be a firefighter. The ones that think they know everything and have a total grip on their abilities are the ones that either get killed or gets you killed. You're going to do well. After all, I'm your FTO. Don't forget it."

The sound of loud varying tones was followed by the crackle of the intercom.

"Station Three – tractor trailer fire at 3131 North West Drive – heavy smoke showing – 21:00."

"FNG, get your gear and get your ass on the rig."

TWENTY-FOUR

....

REVELATION

The sun broke through the curtain and Marine rolled over in bed. She was still sore. But, she was thankful she had the next two days off to replace being called into work unexpectedly. She had spent the last two days adjusting to her new memories. While working, she had thought about her future. She decided that regardless of the outcome that she needed to move on. There was no reason she could think of for finding people she knew before. Her life was in New Brook.

Hearing a knock on her door, she walked to it to open it. She paused. Thinking better of it, she decided she should check to see who it was.

"Yes?"

"Marine, it is Chet. May I come in?"

"Sure." She opened the door. "I probably look like a rug. I haven't combed my hair yet. Give me a few minutes. Help yourself to making us some coffee. I'll be right back."

Chet went into the kitchen while she looked in the mirror, splashed water on her face, and straightened her clothes a little.

"The coffee should be ready in a few minutes," Chet said as he sat down in a chair.

"Good. I'm going to need it. What's up?" She walked into the kitchen.

Chet got up and followed. "I did not get to speak with you when you came in this morning. Did you sleep in your clothes?"

Marine placed two cups, sugar, and cream along with two spoons on the counter.

"Yes, I did. I was drained. I plan on getting cleaned up before I go over to see Aunt Betsy. Fix your coffee the way you like it. Do you want a full cup?"

"Yes. It is good you are planning to change. She likes her family to look sharp." The thought of being called part of Chet's family brought a smile to Marine's face. He continued, "I wanted to know how your ordeal at work went. How are you?"

"I'm fine. You make a good cup of Joe." Chet took a drink. "They accepted my report. They did interview me. I was a little nervous, but I think they knew that was to be expected since I'd not been in a fatal fire like that one before. It appears to be all good."

"I take it by your answer that you chose not to tell them more than you were asked."

"That's exactly what I did. I felt there was no sense in stirring the pot." Marine smiled as she thought of a witch stirring a pot to conjure up some magical potion. "I've decided to let my past be my past. My plans are to stay in New Brook. Who knows, I might even consider going into fire investigations. I'm happy here. Now that Ana-Geliza is gone. I'm ready to look to the future."

"Are you ready to talk with me about what happened with her?"

"No. Not yet. But, there will be a time that I will."

Chet smiled, got up out of his chair, walked over to Marine and patted her on the shoulder, and then turned to go out the door. He stopped and turned back. "I want to encourage you to take some time before you begin making any definite plans. You need to make sure you know what you want before you make your next move. You will not like this idea, but I think that you should talk to Drake. He could help. You do know that any time you want to talk, to let your feelings out, I am here for you."

"Thanks, Chet. I'm thankful for you and blessed to have you and Aunt Betsy in my life. It means a lot to me to know I have a home here."

"You get changed. I know Aunt Betsy has prepared you something to eat. See you in a bit." He closed the door.

Marine sat there for about five minutes and thought about the last seventy-two hours as she sipped the last of her cup of coffee. She couldn't have imagined all that had happened. She wasn't sure she wanted to think about it anymore, but she knew that if she didn't face her demons—those from her old life—she could go crazy.

After she showered and changed, Marine made her way over to the house. This time, instead of walking straight to the back door, she meandered through the garden that separated the house from the cottage apartment she now called her own. She could see Aunt Betsy working in the kitchen. She walked along the paths of the garden looking at the different beds. Aunt Betsy put a lot of work into her vegetable and herb garden. It was clear she loved it. She needed to find something to love with as much passion. She needed to move forward and not look back.

Marine walked into the kitchen that was warm and cozy. She hugged herself; it felt like home. She wanted to stay there and not face the world.

"There you are. Good morning, Marine," Aunt Betsy placed a pan of homemade biscuits into the oven. "Are you ready for a late breakfast or would you like some lunch?"

Marine looked at the clock; it was a little after noon. "Good morning." She walked over to Aunt Betsy, placed her arm around her shoulder, and said, "How about I have some of that fresh bread when it comes out of the oven with some of your homemade jam or fresh honey?"

Aunt Betsy looked up and smiled. "You know, you can have whatever you want. Chet told me that things went pretty well for you during your interview after that horrible fire. It's a shame you are having such a trial. I know it can be hard, but this too will pass." She turned and gave Marine a hug. The strength in her arms told Marine that she meant what she said.

"Thanks, Aunt Betsy. You seem to have an insight into me that no one else seems to have. You give me confidence." Marine walked over to the counter, poured coffee into her cup. "What are you doing today?"

"After I finish fixing you something to eat, I'm going to bake a couple of sugar pumpkins. Then, I'll prepare the puree so that I can have fresh pumpkin to make some pumpkin soup and maybe a pumpkin pie. If I have enough, I'd like to make my famous pumpkin pie bars. You know the ones you loved at Thanksgiving."

"Thanksgiving? That seems ages ago. What day is it today anyway? I've gotten messed up with going to work to cover for Doc."

"Why Marine, it is December thirtieth. Tomorrow is New Year's Eve."

"Wow, time sure seems to be flying. I can't seem to figure it out. Time never used to be so fast for me. Course, I hated my life then."

Aunt Betsy turned around and leaned against the counter. She placed her hands inside her apron pockets.

The Fire of Revenge

Marine decided to confide in Aunt Betsy. "Did Chet tell you I had regained my memory?"

"No, dear, he didn't. I must say you are pretty calm having had such an experience."

"You didn't see me in the hours right after. I was not so calm."

"What happened? Was it during the fire?" Aunt Betsy stared, and then Marine saw the look of realization come over her face. "You saw your past *in* the fire."

"You could say that. There was someone at the fire who wanted to kill me. It was Ana-Geliza. I think she set the fire on purpose knowing if she made it big enough that Station Three would be called. She almost killed my partner, Fish, too."

"How are you doing with it?"

"I'm still coming to grips with some of it. Ana-Geliza and I fought. During the struggle, my memory began to come back. As she went over the edge of the elevator shaft, something flashed and I knew everything about my past. And Ana-Geliza was gone, again."

"Do you want to talk about what you remember?"

"One day, when I have the courage, I'll tell you more about my past, but not now. And, I've not told Chet about fighting Ana-Geliza."

"Why?"

"I don't know. I wasn't ready when he was at the cottage a little while ago."

"What made you ready to tell me?"

"It's hard to explain. It felt right that I tell you. I guess because I felt you would understand."

"Are you going to tell him?"

"Yes, at some point. But, for now, I'd like to keep it between you and me."

"Marine, may I be frank with you?"

"Sure."

"You have had a blow to your mind having your memory come back so strong and under such a harsh way. But, it shouldn't mean that the life you led before wasn't valuable or necessary."

"Aunt Betsy. How can you possibly say that? You have no idea the kind of life I lived."

"Well, now. I'm not so sure I can't imagine it. I mean. I know from my own experiences that you had a dangerous job. You probably worked with strange and cruel people."

"How could you know any of that? Did Chet tell you?"

"No. He has kept your confidence. I know by the way you carry yourself and how you react to things. You, my dear, don't know everything about my past or me either. You shouldn't assume that I've always lived a simple life here in New Brook."

"But, you would not understand. You cannot imagine the things I did in the name of the job."

"You can tell me what you feel comfortable telling me when you are ready. But, I will tell you something about my past that may help you." Marine looked up from her cup of coffee. "I worked for an agency in D.C. I did covert operations. And I am not proud of all of the things I was involved in—but they were necessary in order to protect our country and our freedom."

"Are you saying what I think you are saying?"

"Marine, I am telling you I worked for the INR. Intelligence and research—within the Department of State—I was tasked with analyzing information."

"What?" Marine about choked as her mouth suddenly dropped open.

"Yes. Yes, I did. Now, is there anything you can tell me that is any more shocking?"

"I was an agent for a company called TRANS."

"You were an assassin hired by TRANS to do very dangerous jobs."

"How—"

"Remember who I worked for. I knew about TRANS and companies like them when you were just a little girl."

"I can see how you must have."

"Now, can you say that the people you killed deserved to die? No, you can't. But, you did your job as you had been trained. You were a machine doing a job. Does that mean you were not a good person? No. It means you did your job. You have since learned that you want a different life. You know you can be someone else. Now, you need to learn how to live with your past and allow your soul to heal. No different than a soldier or a police officer having to do his or her duty."

Marine nodded. She heard Aunt Betsy's words. Yet, she doubted them. She doubted herself, too.

The Fire of Revenge

"I've never doubted myself before. I was always strong and sure. Now, I feel like a royal wimp—like a Probie." Marine smiled, as Fish came to mind. His and Aunt Betsy's words were resonating with her.

"Don't doubt yourself. You're all you've got between sanity and insanity. Knowing who you are and who you want to be is the difference."

"You're right, Aunt Betsy. You are good for me." Marine got up and walked over to her. "May I get another hug? I think I could use it right now."

"Sure, sweetie."

The silence was broken by the sound of the phone.

"Hello?" Aunt Betsy laid her dishtowel down on the counter. "Yes, she is right here." She handed Marine the phone. "It's Drake."

TWENTY-FIVE

....

LET HIM GO

As Marine drove to meet Drake, she thought about Aunt Betsy working for the INR. That was not something she would have expected hearing from a petite, artful woman. With the world changing around her at every turn, Marine wondered why she was going to see Drake. He had begged her to come. She tried to back out. But she needed to let him know her memory was back. She had to admit, she couldn't wait to see the look on his face. He did sound like it was urgent. She wondered what was so important.

She parked the Jeep, gathered her coat, and walked into Belle's. At least, they were meeting at a location where she knew some friendly faces, she thought as she went through the door.

"Hello, Marine," Belle said as she walked toward her. She pulled Marine into a hug and said, "I've missed seeing you. Have a seat here. You will enjoy my new soup I've made."

"Oh thanks, Belle. Just bring me some hot tea. I'm meeting someone here and I'm not sure if we'll eat. Is that okay?"

"Sure, sweetie. Drake will probably eat."

"How'd you know who was coming?"

"Good guess." She smiled and walked away.

Drake came in through the front door; Marine waved to him. As he walked up to her, memories of their time on the cruise ship flashed across her eyes.

"You look hot. Are you okay?" Drake said as he pulled up a seat.

"Hello, to you, too." She put her hand to her cheek. "I'm not too warm."

"No, silly. I meant you look good." He smiled with a look that made her heart melt. She had an urge to take him right there in front of everyone. One thing gaining her memory back had done for her was to give her back a sense of desire for Drake that she liked.

"How have you been?" she asked, changing the subject.

"I've been okay. I understand you had a working K fire the other night. Do you know who died?"

"You know that I do."

Drake moved his chair closer to the table. Belle walked up with Marine's hot tea. "Would you like some coffee?" Drake nodded.

"So, how long have you been coming in here?"

"Ever since the night of your party after graduation."

Marine looked him over. "Drake. I have my memory back."

"I figured you might regain it if you ran into Ana-Geliza."

"You aren't surprised?"

"No. Why? What did you expect after we told you Ana-Geliza was gunning for you?"

"Don't say her name so loud."

"You can't be afraid. Not the strong and powerful, Marine."

"You're not cute."

"What am I then?"

"Exasperating."

He smiled. "Look. The reason I wanted you to meet is that I needed to catch you up on events. Before the other night's fire, I was going to tell you some things about Ana-Geliza. Now, I need to let you know what is happening in the world in which you used to travel."

"How do you know what happened?"

"Please. I am MI6. You do remember that, don't you?"

"Drake, I'm not sure I want to return to that life."

He looked at Marine, looked around, and leaned in closer to her. "You realize you may not have a choice."

"Yes. I know that."

"You also realize you could be putting those you've come to love in danger."

"Actually, I have thought of that, too. I figured that if they think my memory is still gone, any of TRANS past agents or companies like them will continue to leave me alone. They have so far. I'm hoping to disappear into the woodwork around here."

"If I and the other agent could find you—yes, I won't mention her name—then you know others from TRANS who have gone to work elsewhere can find you, if they feel they should." He stopped talking for effect. "That's why I wanted to talk with you. I received news you may find useful to your future."

The Fire of Revenge

Marine wondered if he was there for her benefit or for his own. "Okay. What do you have to tell me?"

He took Marine's hand and held it with care. "Marine, I want to explain some things."

"Excuse me," Belle said. "Would you like something to eat?" Drake let go of Marine's hand.

"No, I'm not hungry right now," Marine looked up at Belle. She saw Belle was staring at Drake.

"How about you?" Drake looked at Marine, and then at Belle.

"Would you mind bringing my usual, Belle?"

"Sure. I'm at your service." She walked away.

"What's with her? She didn't sound as friendly as before."

Drake shrugged. "I guess coming here wasn't such a good idea after all. I didn't realize Belle would be so possessive."

"Why is she acting like that? Have you two gotten close?"

"Yes. When I saw you weren't all that interested in me, I made a play for her. She evidently fell hard."

"Looking at her now, watching you and me, she is green with envy. And, I'll be honest. I understand why. I do remember our time on the ship. You are something worth being jealous over." This time Drake blushed. Marine smiled.

"We need to talk about TRANS. I'll blurt this out so we can get on with next steps. As you know, since TRANS has folded, you might be safe. But, you might be a target for some countries."

"What?"

"With the change in government policies, cutbacks, economies of different countries going sour, the need for companies like TRANS began to dry up about a year ago. And, to top it off, there were some smartasses who decided to share their secrets and sensitive material that when revealed, caused governments to distance themselves from companies like TRANS. Many of the contracts TRANS completed were often illegal. In effect, TRANS was disavowed."

Marine realized if TRANS was in trouble a year ago, it was while she was on the cruise. "I had no idea."

"You wouldn't have known about it. TRANS kept you in the field. But, those in the home office were very aware."

"When did you say that TRANS folded?"

"About the time we were on the ship."

"Why didn't you tell me?

"It happened the day you lost your memory."

"Taking the Galley tour was an all-around bad idea." Marine thought back to that fall and how her entire world had changed. "Now, what happens?"

"That's an important question. I think TRANS folding is what gave Ana-Geliza the enticement that she felt she could come after you. She hated you because she learned you were the operative that did the job when her brother was killed."

"Yeah. I made that connection the other night. I tried to explain it to her, but she was not going to listen to me."

"No. She was one crazy chick. I'm glad you weren't hurt."

"It could have gone either way. We both could have died. I'm glad Fish wasn't caught up in it any more than he was and that he wasn't hurt too badly."

"You were lucky that she didn't shoot you."

"I think she would have, had things gone differently. My ability to fight her with my fire gear on caught her off guard. I think she had plans to take me with her out of the warehouse. Wherever it was she was going to take me, she had plans to take her time with me."

"What makes you think that?"

"It would have been what I would have done."

"Marine?"

"Yes."

"What are you going to do?"

"With TRANS folded, I'm totally free. I think I'm going to stay here. I like it here. And you? What are you going to do?"

"First off, like I said before. I'm not so sure you're totally free. When I get back to London, I plan to make sure your identity is entirely wiped clean from all records. Okay?" Marine nodded. "If I thought we had a chance, I'd ask you to go with me. But, I think you know what we had; it wasn't anything more than lust." Marine nodded. "It was good though."

She smiled and thought about how good it was. "I wouldn't mind revisiting it again." A part of her hoped he'd bite on the idea.

"But, you know we must part ways."

Belle walked up and placed Drake's food hard on the table. He reached up and caught her wrist.

"Belle, have a seat."

"I can't, Drake. I'm working." A customer called for Belle to come over. "Excuse me. Drake, will I see you later?"

"Yes. I'll be back around closing. Okay?"

"Sure."

Drake watched Belle walk away with a quick step. "I will tell Belle later tonight that I am leaving here and heading back to London tomorrow."

"You are saying bye to her on New Year's Eve? How typically MI6 of you."

"Yes. I'm a walking cliché. My work here is done. I need to get back to my job."

"What work did you have here?"

"Protecting you."

"What?"

"When you lost your memory, my assignment changed from stopping you from completing your assassination of Tony to keeping you safe until you regained your memory. I kept my position and job function a secret from you at the encouragement of Chet."

"Chet?"

"Yes. When you were in the infirmary those first hours. I told Chet all about you and your history. I didn't know who would be gunning for you once I heard that TRANS had folded. I had fallen hard for you in those first few days we were together. Marine, I will always cherish you. I love you enough to let you go. You are no longer the same person. We can't stay together. I have a different life than you. You are happy here. Your eyes light up when you talk about being a firefighter. I get that. I want you to love your new life. It is obvious that what you were doing before was causing you to live each moment as though it were your last."

Marine looked deep into Drake's eyes. She saw for the first time an honest, caring soul. "Drake, I'm not sure I even know what to say."

"There is nothing you need to say. Listen to me. Grab this chance you've created. You no longer need or want the life you had before. I can't leave what I do, not yet. So, you need to go forward and not look back. You need to know that no matter where you are or where I am, I will always be there to help and protect you. You remember how to reach me if you ever need me?"

"Yes. Like always, I'm to use the drop box."

"Yes. And one more thing, I'll love you always. Funny. I don't know the reason why. But, I do. I'm proud of you, Marine. Enjoy this

The Fire of Revenge

new life." Drake stood up, took her hand, squeezed it, and then turned and walked over to Belle.

Marine sat there transfixed. She had not realized how her life had become dependent upon him and his protection even though she had resisted any idea of him being involved. His last words made her realize she always knew he was taking care of her back. She wanted to ask him not to leave, but she knew he was right. She had no right to make him stay. She knew that she wouldn't leave. She had made a choice to stay and she was going to see it through.

* * * * *

As Marine drove home, she thought about Drake and what could have been. She turned off Main Street onto Tazewell and heard a car honk behind her. Looking in the rearview mirror, she saw that it was Wayne. Marine drove to the firehouse parking lot. She parked and Wayne pulled in beside her. He motioned for her to join him in his truck.

"You free right now?" he asked as she got into the front seat.

"Yes. Why?"

"I want to take you somewhere. Can you take about an hour?"

"Let me get my purse. I'll be right back." Marine grabbed her bag, locked up the Jeep, and got back in Wayne's truck.

"Where are we going?" Marine fixed her seat belt.

"You'll see."

As they rode, Marine figured she should keep quiet about the last few days. As much as she felt she liked Wayne and wanted to get to know him better, she decided not to tell him her story. He was still her supervisor.

"How are you feeling?"

"I'm a little sore still, but, for the most part, I'm ready to get back to work."

"You've already had more experience in a few days then some rookies get in a month. You should do well in the department as long as you keep your powder dry."

"Okay. I have to ask. Exactly what does that mean?"

"Well, around these parts, it means to stay careful and be ready for a possible emergency."

"I understand the need for being ready and all, but where did the powder part come from?"

The Fire of Revenge

"From what I've been told by some of the old-timers, it refers to keeping your gun powder dry so it would ignite when you needed it. It also goes with trusting in God, so that when you are faced with a life or death situation, no matter what comes your way, you can face the situation. You need to be confident, hope for the best, and be prepared for the worst."

"All of that out of those four little words? You are full of information, aren't you?"

"Actually, I am. Here we are."

Marine looked around and realized Wayne had driven into a part of the county she had not seen before. In front of the truck was a pristine lake. The water was as still as though it was a mirror. The reflections of the trees that lined the banks seemed perfect. As she studied the water, she felt serene. If she didn't know for sure her location, she'd think she was looking at the trees upside down. It was peaceful. They got out of the truck and walked to the water's edge. The only sound was a light breeze blowing the grasses along one side of the bank.

"What are you doing?" Wayne asked as he walked toward her. "You look like you're trying to stand on your head."

"I'm checking out the trees' reflections." She had bent down and tried to look at the trees upside down in order to see if the reflections looked different.

"Come on. I want to show you something."

They walked for a while, along the edge of the lake. Then, they walked through a grove of trees.

"What is this place?"

"It's my property. I'm thinking about building a house here someday."

"Really. How much land do you own?"

"About a hundred acres give or take a few."

"What? How will you use this land?"

"I don't plan to use it. I plan to live on it."

"Okay," Marine's subconscious could not relate to someone who wanted to own land for the sake of it. "I didn't mean anything by that. Most people buy land, and then use it."

"Sure they do. But, then they ruin it."

"Yes. That they do."

They walked for another two hundred or so yards, and then Wayne stopped and turned toward her.

"Now, I want you to sit down right here." He spread out a blanket he had been carrying. "We will sit here and talk."

The Fire of Revenge

"Wish you'd brought some wine and cheese."

"Does everything always have to be a party with you?"

"Whoa, Wayne. I didn't mean anything by that. I just thought it was a lovely, romantic location. Why are you so tense? And, anyway, it's New Year's Eve. I can't help to be a little excited."

"I guess I should explain." He looked down at his hands, and then looked out at the water. "We decided together when you got hired on to the station that we wouldn't be able to have a relationship." He stopped and looked at her. She felt his eyes pierce her soul. "But, things have changed as of today."

"Why?"

"I know you are aware of the department's policy that frowns on relationships between firefighters and their supervisors. But, what you might not be aware of is the fact we can see each other as long as I'm in a different division or department."

"What are you trying to tell me?"

"I'm leaving Station Three."

"You can't leave firefighting. It's your whole life. What will you do? Who'll be our Captain?"

"I'm not leaving firefighting. I'm moving on to another division. I'll be moving into the position of Battalion Chief."

"Really? When?"

"First of the year, tomorrow." Wayne smiled at Marine. "Don't you have something to say?"

"I'm trying to wrap my mind around this. You're telling me that we will be able to date if we want?"

"If we want."

Marine smiled and looked off in the distance. She couldn't believe how her life was taking a turn. For a moment, if she confided in Wayne, how would it hurt? But then, she could hear Drake and Chet's words warning her not to tell anyone, ever.

"What will happen? Who will be our Captain?"

"I'm not sure. It is part of my job to make a recommendation. I'm still thinking that through. But, what about us?"

"Well, I don't know. This is good to hear."

"You're being cautious."

"Sure. I don't want to get my hopes up."

"Okay, let's take it slow then."

"That would be best."

"I need to ask you something else."

"Okay."

"What do you think about moving into management?"

"Fire management?"

"Yes."

"I'm not sure about that. I have been thinking about fire investigations, though. These last few fires have given me a taste of what it's like to work an arson fire. And, after watching a couple of television shows, I'm thinking I should check into my options."

"There's plenty of potential for growth on the fire investigation and bomb squad team. You should consider it. Especially now, with the openings coming up—several of the upper group are retiring and two were injured in a car wreck last week. You'd be able to move right into a position once you graduated."

"How long is the training?"

"Let's see, I think it is only four weeks. You can do most of it online. You will need to do onsite training at a couple of different locations in order to acquire your police powers and pass a final exam. And, unlike what was done with your basic training acceptance, you will need to have an extensive background check with the state police."

Marine shot a look at Wayne. Oh God, she thought. She would need Drake's assistance a lot quicker than she expected. Wayne continued talking as they walked to his truck. She didn't half hear him as she thought about her next moves.

"Marine." She stopped walking and looked at him. "Did you hear me?"

"Ah, no. I'm sorry. I was in deep thought."

"Yeah. I could see that. I asked if you'd go to dinner with me tonight. We could kick off the New Year together."

Marine smiled. Life was turning out to be good after all.

TWENTY-SIX

....

FACING FIENDS

The next month, Marine saw many changes take place at Station Three. The first week of January, Captain Wayne left to begin his service as Battalion Chief. He and Marine began to see each other a couple of times a week. His replacement, Captain Sam Bottoms, came from the administrative side of the New Brook Fire Department. There was much speculation as to what kind of job Captain Bottoms would perform.

Marine had started the fire investigations training that first week, too, which allowed her to miss Captain Bottoms' arrival. Now, with only ten days left of training, she hoped her assignment to fire investigations would come through before she had to find out if the things she'd heard about him were true. The last ten days of training, she would be going to different classes around the region to interact with other fire investigators and to receive practical experience. It allowed some free time to visit different firehouses along the way as she traveled to her next class. She decided to drop by the Station Three firehouse to catch up with a few of the guys on her way to one of those classes.

"Hello, Letsco," Crab and Fish called to Marine.

"Grab yourself some coffee and come sit," Fish said as he moved his chair aside for her.

"It's good to be back in the firehouse. How are you guys?" Marine set her coffee down and reached for the sugar.

"We're good. How's fire investigation training going?"

"I've got eight days left. Is there anything to eat?"

"Sure. We've got granola bars, grapes, and all kinds of healthy food." Crab walked over to the refrigerator and pulled out a tray of donuts. "Look at these. They're made with whole grains and sugar-free icing." We laughed.

"I'm sure these are healthy. What's going on?"

The Fire of Revenge

"It's Captain Bottoms' new plan to keep us in shape." Fish winked at Marine.

"Really. So, I take it what I've heard is true."

"It is worse," Crab pulled his chair in closer to the table.

"I guess it's good I'm not here."

"You've got that right." Fish looked at the door. He whispered, "I'd not be surprised if we found this place bugged."

Marine smiled but saw that Fish and Crab looked grave. "It's changed that much?"

"Worse. He's messing everything up. He has no practical experience. He's never fought a fire. All he knows is management."

"Based on how you guys feel about him, his management skills must be lacking, too."

"Letsco," Captain Sam Bottoms called for her as he walked into the kitchen.

"Yes, sir."

"Why are you here? You're supposed to be at class in Evansham today, are you not?"

"Yes."

"Then, you should get going."

Marine winked at Crab and Fish, "I'll see you guys later. Thank you, Captain."

"Letsco, before you go, I need to see you in my office."

"Yes, sir." Marine followed him across the hall.

In his office, she was taken back. He had stripped the walls of the fire department pictures Captain Wayne had displayed. The room was clean and void of any semblance that had once showed fire department pride. In its place, hung three stark pictures of samurais. The room appeared dogmatic and cold. Captain Bottoms motioned for her to sit.

He stood before her and tapped his pencil on his desk. "You're still assigned to me and I have some rules you need to follow." He pointed to the pictures behind him. "Take a good look at these pictures. You'll notice each one shows a different mood. The thing you need to remember is the one that is in the center is the mood that I am in for that day. So, if you want to know how I may react to a screw up you or your shift makes, just walk in here and see which picture is in the middle. You'll know."

Marine looked at him and tried to keep her mouth from falling open. Was he for real?

He continued, "Just because you made it through The Academy with high honors doesn't mean I'm going to cut you any slack.

And, just because you're in training with fire investigations doesn't mean I won't watch every move you make when you try to make my department look bad. You understand me?"

"Yes, sir. Perfectly." Marine got up, walked to the door, turned around, and said, "I'm heading to class now. You have a good day."

As Marine walked to her Jeep, she tried her best not to let him get under her skin. Crab and Fish were right; he was indeed a royal pain and maybe just a tad crazy.

* * * * *

A few days later, while Marine was getting ready for one of her last classes, she broke a fingernail back to the cuticle.

"Aunt Betsy?" Marine walked into the kitchen.

"Yes, dear. Are you leaving now?"

"In a bit. I've broken a nail."

"Child, you've done more than that. Sit here. I'll get my first aid kit. It's bleeding pretty bad."

After Aunt Betsy had cleaned and bandaged her finger, she said, "You need to go see Crystal. She'll patch your broken nail and will protect your others by painting them with this new gel polish she's gotten in stock. It will make your nails more durable. I'll call her and see when she can work you in, okay?" Aunt Betsy began dialing the phone.

"Sure. It would be nice to have nails. Besides, I don't want to break any more and have my fingers hurting during my last days of class."

"Crystal said she can see you after four today. I told her you'd call her if it didn't work."

"Thanks, Aunt Betsy. It will work fine. See you later." Marine gave her a kiss and headed to work.

* * * * *

Marine walked into Crystal's Shaping Nail Salon promptly at four in the afternoon.

"Hello, may I help you?" The lady behind the counter had long red hair and sparkling blue eyes.

"I'm Marine. Aunt Betsy sent me."

"Oh, hello. I'm Crystal. Come on in here to my nail salon table. Let me see that finger nail you hurt."

Marine walked in, placed her bag down on the chair next to the table, and showed Crystal, her hand. The room was laid out to do nails and there was a pedicure area. "You do toes, too?"

"Yes, we do. You did a job on that nail. But we'll be able to fix it. Now, what color would you like me to use?"

"That's a great question. I don't know. What choices do I have?"

"Look over there on the wall. We can use any one of the twelve on the bottom shelf. You do want me to use the gel polish, right?"

"Yes, I believe so. What is this gel polish?"

"Oh, it's a nifty way to help your nails last a long time without breaking. The gel gives a very resilient protection for your nails. I will polish them, cure them using a special light, and then you will have beautiful nails that will last at least three weeks, no matter what you do."

"Well, that's cool. I need it with all of the messy work I'm doing."

Crystal began to work on Marine's nails. They talked about Marine's job while Crystal cleaned, soaked, and then began to polish them. She was in the midst of polishing her left hand when they heard a loud noise in the reception area.

Crystal got up and peered around the corner of the door. She turned back to Marine. She whispered, "It's my ex-husband George and his brother."

"What do you think you're doing?" Crystal said as she walked up to them. Marine followed close behind.

"Shut up, bitch. You could get hurt."

Marine saw that they had their hands in the cash drawer.

"It looks like you have your fingers in the wrong drawers."

"You mean drawer, don't you?"

"No." He swung at Marine, but she managed to step aside. In one quick move, she caught his arm, spun him around, and knee kicked him in his tailbone. He fell to the floor. The second guy ran away before Marine could turn to him.

Crystal helped Marine pick up the fallen man. "George, are you insane trying to rob me?" George jerked his arm away.

Marine shoved him toward the door. "Go on. Get out of here. And, if you come back, I'll tell all your friends that you got whipped by a girl." George stumbled out the door.

"Oh wow! Thank you, Marine. You were magnificent!"

The Fire of Revenge

"It was nothing. I haven't had a hard day's work since yesterday."

"It looks like you broke another nail on your unpolished hand."

"It's a shame we didn't have them all done in time. At least, I know that gel stuff works." They laughed.

* * * * *

After helping Crystal clean up her shop, Marine paid her and left for Chet's office. When she pulled up to his office building, she wondered if he was free. She saw his vehicle parked across the street.

Knocking at Chet's door, Marine walked on in not waiting for him to respond.

"Hello, Marine. Welcome to my new digs, by the way."

"This is nice, Chet. Have I caught you at a bad time?"

"No. I was finishing up some notes and was going to head over to a special Rotary dinner. How are you this evening?"

"I've had better days. It seems this is my week for running into fiends of all sorts."

"Really. Like whom?"

"My boss for one."

"Your boss? Wayne?"

"No. My new boss, Captain Sam Bottoms. He is a samurai enthusiast."

"You mean a bushido?"

"I'm not familiar with that word."

"This is a term for the way of the warrior. It is supposed to convey what the samurai believed."

"Captain Bottoms clearly has a warped sense of samurai principles then."

"Why do you say that?"

Marine explained his use of the samurai pictures.

Chet walked across the room and turned back toward Marine. "He does indeed have a warped sense of honor and duty to his Lord, the fire department, even without any regard to whether or not he causes suffering to others."

"How do I handle him?"

"Keep your distance as much as possible and be prepared." Chet looked at his watch. "It's getting close to time. Do you want to resume talking later?"

"No. Let me think about what you've said. I'll see you later. Have fun."

"You too. Tell Aunt Betsy I'll see her tomorrow."

The Fire of Revenge

Marine nodded and pulled the door behind her. Great, she thought, as she walked toward her Jeep. Just what she needed, a crazy boss.

She drove to Trout House Falls, parked her car at the back next to the cottage, and walked into the house. She found Aunt Betsy sitting on the couch in the den. "Hey," Marine said as she sat down beside her. "What are you doing?"

"I thought I'd work on my knitting."

"I didn't realize you knitted, too."

"I don't get to very often. But, you didn't come in here to talk about my knitting. What's up?"

"I guess I'm scared. I had to face some evil souls today. I thought I'd not have to deal with that sort of thing now that I have left TRANS and Ana-Geliza is dead."

She walked over to the fireplace and began to twirl the poker around in its rack.

"Something else?"

"Why do you ask?"

"You're playing with the fireplace poker."

"I'm sorry. I guess I'm thinking about what happened at Crystal's."

"That's right. Let me see those lovely nails. Red. How fitting for you."

"Thanks. I thought since we're almost into February and it being heart month and all, I'd get a color that would work."

"They do look lovely. Now, you were talking about being scared and evil souls. I'm here to tell you that the world is full of evil. And, sadly, we don't have to look far."

"I guess I was hoping my life would be easier and I wouldn't have to face any more demons or figure out what I can or cannot do. I just want to do it—like what happened at Crystal's."

"You said that before. You got your nails polished."

"That isn't all that happened."

"Well, do tell."

Marine went on to explain how Crystal's ex-husband had come into the shop to rob her and how she had managed to chase the man and his brother out of the shop. "I'm not sure I want it to get out that I can handle myself. How would I explain it? I mean, how would I explain to the guys at work that I'm trained in different defense tactics? No one knows about my past. I'd like to keep it that way."

"You raise some important questions. I faced some of those when I first moved back here. It's funny how people think you have a particular past based on how you behave and react to things now. They never know what you have experienced or where your life had taken you before you came here. I guess I'm saying, don't worry about what you are going to get; be happy for what you have. Most importantly, wish for what you want."

"You're saying I shouldn't be fearful of my future—I can have my dream. And to not worry."

"Yes. It is that simple. As for people finding out about your abilities, don't worry about that either. Use them when you need them. God saw to it that you should have these talents for a reason."

"Have I told you how much I love you?"

"Not enough."

TWENTY-SEVEN

....

BURNING REVENGE

Ana-Geliza rolled over onto her side. A sharp pain shot through her shoulder and down her back. She winced in pain.

"I'm going to kill her."

"Who?"

"The same bitch I've talked about since Christmas. You know who."

"Tell me again. I want to hear the anger in your voice."

"Marine Letsco. I'm going to kill Marine Letsco."

"That's my girl."

"How much longer will I be laid up in this rat hole?"

"Not long. You've been recuperating well. Another week or so, you should be able to move around well enough."

"Enough to fight?"

"Most likely."

"How do you know so much about doctoring anyway?"

"I was in medical school until I decided I needed a warmer profession that would give me a chance to awaken and excite the flame in me."

"You really *like* fire."

"Yes, a *lot*."

Ana-Geliza rose up on the bed. "God, I hate this place. I'm getting cabin fever."

"Take it easy. If it wasn't for me, you'd be in jail or dead."

"Why do you deserve such credit?"

"I got you off the top of that elevator and into my car. It was the corpse I put in your place they found and not your scorched body. Without me, you'd not be able to complete your plans. Don't worry. Marine will find the clue I left just as you instructed."

TWENTY-EIGHT

....

IT'S NOT WHAT IT SEEMS

While studying for her final exam, Marine reread a sentence about fire investigations.

Law enforcement and fire service departments must always determine the cause of the fire whether arson or accidental, in order to identify hazards and dangerous practices and prevent future fires.

Marine put down her pen and looked out the window. All fires have a cause. What about fire deaths? She thought back to the two earlier fatal fires. All fires have a cause—some accidental, some not.

She picked up the pen and began to twirl it like a sixties rock drummer would twirl a drumstick. Each time, the bodies were found after the fire was extinguished. Then, she found the tattoo shape scrawled on the wall. But, with Ana-Geliza, it was different. Was she at those fires, too? Did she set them? She must have been there. Otherwise, Marine wouldn't have found the drawings. They were crudely scrawled. At the last fire, Ana-Geliza died. There was no tattoo shape to be found at the scene. Or was there?

Looking at the clock on her desk, Marine realized she needed to get to the range for her final test using her 40 cal Glock. She had gotten the gun as part of her training to be a fire marshal. She would have police powers when she graduated.

* * * * *

It had felt good to use a gun at the range. Marine parked her Jeep and gathered her tool kit. The instructor was pleased she'd scored a 98. She was disappointed but felt she'd improve with more practice. While going through the maneuvers on the range, Marine had decided she would visit the fire scene.

Stepping over a burnt floor joist that had fallen, Marine carefully made her way to the second floor of the warehouse where she and Ana-Geliza had fought. She wished she'd had a gun then. Ana-Geliza wouldn't have slipped away.

Reaching into her tool kit, she pulled out her camera and pad of paper to take notes. She might as well go through the scene as she'd learned to do as a fire investigator. Who knows, she might find something she could present to her supervisor. Marine couldn't shake the nagging feeling that the fight with Ana-Geliza seemed too cut and dry. It was just too easy.

As she stepped over the debris, she looked around the room and mentally revisited the fight from the stairs where Fish had fallen over to the far side of the warehouse at the elevator shaft. The building had a basement. They were on the second floor when Ana-Geliza fell. It's possible she landed on top of the elevator and not the bottom of the elevator shaft. She'd been hurt but not to the point that she would have died. No different from last time when she landed on top of the lifeboat—like Wile E. Coyote. Marine looked down over the edge of the floor into the pit below. She could see the top of the elevator with the light shining down from her flashlight. Ana-Geliza must have landed on top after all.

Marine made her way back to the stairs and found an opening to the basement. She managed to step through the opening and caught her coat on a hanging wire. She turned; startled, thinking someone had grabbed her. Get a grip, Marine, she chided herself. You're starting to see ghosts.

Standing inside the elevator car, she saw where she could climb up on its top. How convenient that stool was there, she thought as she climbed through the opening. She steadied herself and began to search the top of the elevator car. She had no idea what she was looking for, but her training had told her to consider everything—walls, doors, windows, ceilings, and floors.

Marine began to take pictures of the area. As she focused on the area of the elevator shaft closest to the top of the elevator, a cold chill ran down her back. There it was. The tattoo.

* * * * *

Driving down the driveway to Trout House Falls, Marine hoped she'd find Chet at the house. But, his car wasn't there.

After she had parked her Jeep, she walked over to the cottage and felt another cold chill.

The Fire of Revenge

She didn't like having the feeling of being watched. She turned and looked out into the woods. She couldn't see anyone, but her experience told her it did not mean she wasn't being watched. Marine walked over to the back of the house, up the steps, and opened the door. Aunt Betsy was standing there with a cup of hot tea.

"You're a mind reader," Marine said as she slowly closed the door behind her. "How'd you know I'd need that right now?"

"I saw you pull up. And when you headed this way, I figured I'd greet you with something warm. You shot out of here earlier like you had something serious on your mind. Now, looking at your clothes, I'd say you found something serious."

"I had forgotten about the final range test. It's hard to believe I'll be an official fire investigator this time tomorrow."

"I'm sure the touch of the gun felt good as it worked in your hand again. It's been a long time."

"Yes. Do you still shoot?"

"I try to go out and practice on the back forty every so often. It's important not to let your aim get weak."

"Would you like to go to the range with me sometime? You could see how well you do when being timed with the long-range targets. It might be fun to see what you can still do."

"It might be fun at that. So, why are your clothes all covered in soot? It looks like you also have been to a fire scene."

"I have."

"Can you tell me about it?"

"Aunt Betsy, I'm not sure I should bring you into this. It really isn't official and I don't want you to get caught up in the middle of something that could be dangerous."

"You are kidding, right?" Aunt Betsy set a plate of cookies on the table as she sat down. "Come over here and sit down. You and I need to talk."

"How long has it been since you've been in the middle of something dangerous?"

"Not as long as you might think. Besides, if you're talking to me, it doesn't mean I'm in the middle of anything. I make a good sounding board. What's going on?"

Marine explained to Aunt Betsy about the tattoo drawings she had found at the previous fire scenes. "I was curious. So I decided to go check out the elevator shaft where Ana-Geliza died."

"Let me guess. You found the tattoo on the wall."

"Yes. There is no way that Ana-Geliza would have known that a body would be found, let alone her own body. How did the drawing of the tattoo get there? Who else knew her plans?"

"Indeed." Aunt Betsy twisted her napkin into a spiral. "You are right to be concerned. None of this fits with Ana-Geliza dying. Are you sure she is dead? You thought she was last time."

Marine nodded her head. "Unlike last time, I had Drake; he knew she was alive. This time, I'm not so certain. Her fall down the elevator shaft was only about fifteen feet. If she lived, she had to have broken something. But, the whole place was on fire. How did she get out?"

"Are you sure it was on fire when she went into the basement? Maybe the fire had not reached that point. Do you know from where it started?"

"You know, you're right. It started on the second floor, where we fought. It would have spread up before it would move downward. If Ana-Geliza managed to get off the top of the elevator car, she could have made it out. But, if that happened, whose body did they find?"

"This is all speculation. You need to get proof."

"How? We don't know anything about Ana-Geliza. Besides, where would she be now? If she were hurt, she'd have to be holing up somewhere recuperating. That would explain why we haven't heard from her since that night. But, with time, she'd be healed. We should be hearing from her soon if she's alive."

"So, then, we need to be prepared. We need to be ready for her to come out of nowhere."

"You're right. But, I'm also worried about who's helping her. She'd need someone to help her. How else would she get food or get around?" Marine shook her head as she thought about possibilities. "We're still missing a key piece."

"When did all of this start?"

"At that first fire when I found the tattoo drawn on the wall above where the body was found. I had my suspicions then, but my memory wasn't fully back. I just knew it couldn't have been a coincidence."

"Then, you've got to go back and relook at the evidence. You should know that all evidence leads you to your prime suspect. You were trained well to avoid leaving evidence. Ana-Geliza was too. But, she has allowed this to get personal. Maybe she has made a mistake along the way."

Bingo.

TWENTY-NINE

ANGER MOUNTS

Her anger mounted to a boiling point as she looked at the smile on Marine's face. Ana-Geliza crumbled the Wednesday issue of the New Brook Times into a tight ball.

"I'm going to kill her and all her little friends, too."

"You're letting that headline get to you. Why?"

"She didn't solve anything. She doesn't know crap about investigations just because she's graduating from four weeks of training. I'm still here. She didn't get rid of me and she doesn't even know where I am. But, I'm going to see to it I get rid of her. Did you get the stuff?"

"No."

"What? Why not? I can't make my next move without it."

"There were cops all over the place. Besides, I don't think you should get the old woman. Let's just burn her house down right there with her in it. That'll fix the broad. She'll really hurt then. She won't have a place to live."

"Are you freaking stupid? We've got to do this just right."

"Oh, crap. The little woman is pissed. If it weren't for me, you'd be dead. I saved your skinny ass and you owe me. I've not been able to do any of the other sparks I'd planned on doing. Now, I'm behind with my own work. Sit down. Take a load off."

Ana-Geliza walked behind him and decided she could kill him right there, but thought better of it. It would be a waste of manpower.

"Listen. I've got an idea. I will go with you to your next spark. I'll help you set up the scene and teach you how to use the timed delay device I've used on several jobs."

"Would you really?" Ana-Geliza smiled. "Wow. Sorry 'bout before. I didn't mean nothing, you know."

"Sure. I understand."

THIRTY

....

CLUE

The Wednesday morning ceremonies of Marine and the other trainees graduating from the fire investigation school were over by ten. It was simple with the six graduates receiving a certificate of completion. As Marine looked her certificate, a sense of pride came over her. She was officially a fire marshal for the New Brook Fire Department, her new title as a fire investigator.

At the firehouse, she went to her locker and began to organize her things. She had been told she would need to be issued new gear and a new set of uniforms. She had barely gotten her existing ones broken in, she thought as she moved them onto the rack.

"Letsco." Marine turned to see Captain Bottoms standing before her. "I have your orders here. You are to report to the Chief Fire Marshal Edwin Altizer's office at eleven this morning."

"Yes, sir."

"I would say I was happy for you, but I don't know you. Let's hope you can do a good job." Captain Bottoms turned around and walked off.

Marine saluted him but didn't feel he deserved it. The sad part was leaving the guys. But, Fish and Crab would educate the Captain before all was said and done.

"FNG!" Fish called as he walked up to her, and then pulled her into his arms. "I guess you're on your way. I knew you'd make it in this career. I guess I shouldn't call you FNG anymore, but it will always be my nickname for you. When do you head up on the hill?"

"I have to report to Chief Altizer's at eleven."

"You better get going, it's ten forty-five now."

"Okay. See ya, Fish. You will tell the—"

"Yeah. Get out of here. I know what to tell them."

* * * * *

Chief Altizer stood up from his desk as Marine walked in. He extended his hand. "Glad to meet you, Fire Marshal Letsco. Welcome to the Fire Investigations and Bomb Squad department."

"Glad to be here, sir." Marine smiled. He appeared to be a career man with a few years from retirement as gray hair colored his temples. He had on a crisply ironed long-sleeve dress white uniform shirt with a gold badge, bugles on the collar, and a gold nameplate tucked neatly in black dress pants. His shoes were shiny black patent leather. He took pride in how he looked.

"Have a seat. I want to take you around and introduce you to the other fire marshals that are on shift and fill you in on a few cases we're working on. I also want you to understand that just because you are young in experience doesn't mean we don't expect great things out of you. You graduated top in your fire marshal class just like you did with your firefighter training. You have a real knack for this work. We're glad to have you on board."

"Thank you, sir. I'm proud to be a part of this team."

"Let's go meet the other guys. It will be good to have a female touch around here."

Marine wondered if he meant that as a compliment or if she'd be taking notes, fetching coffee, or serving as all-around gopher. She would have to break a case real soon to avoid that from happening, she thought as they walked to greet her co-workers.

First, she was introduced to Fire Marshal Pike.

"Just call me Matt."

"Hello, sir."

"You're the firefighter I met when we did the debrief at Station Three." Pike stood about five foot seven, red hair, and broad shoulders. His uniform mirrored Chief Altizer's, but it wasn't as sharp.

"Yes."

"Glad to have you on board."

Chief Altizer led Marine to several other desks and said, "You know all three of the fatal fires you worked are still open. Maybe you can work on them, too."

"Yes, sir. Thank you. It would be a challenge and one I welcome."

Then, Marine was introduced to Fire Marshal Tom Willard. He was tall, about six foot two, his dark black hair had gray mixed along the sides. He reminded Marine of a cross

The Fire of Revenge

between Tom Hanks and Sean Connery. He looked like he knew more than he would say, yet was willing to try things that were not always within the rulebook. His desk was filled with piles of paperwork.

"Ignore my stacks. I can find anything as long as no one moves my stacks." They laughed and shook hands. "Glad to meet you."

"You, too."

"Now, let me show you your desk," Chief Altizer pointed to a typical office desk.

Marine looked the desk over. There was already a pile of files sitting on top. A computer laptop with a desk phone that had an earpiece sat off to one side. To the right of the computer was a printer-fax-copier-scanner all in one. Marine realized her work had already been assigned to her.

"Letsco, you have all you need to begin. I'll leave you to it. If you need anything or have questions, check with Tom, first." Chief Altizer walked away.

"I'll be over here working on some documentation of the latest fire we had last night. We believe it was arson." Tom said as he walked over to his desk.

"Thanks, sir." Marine began to shuffle through the stack of files on her desk.

"You do know you don't have to be formal with me. Call me Tom." He smiled and walked over to his desk.

"Okay, Tom. Thanks." Marine stopped suddenly with her shuffling. Could it be? Surely her luck couldn't be that good right now. Sitting before her were the files of the last three arson fires she had fought as a firefighter—including the one where Ana-Geliza supposedly died.

Marine spent a couple of hours scanning the files and putting them into the database. Each time she scanned the pictures of one of the fire scenes, she studied it carefully. The pictures of the last fire, when Ana-Geliza fell to the top of the elevator car, she had not seen before. She devoted the most time looking them over.

She knew she needed to take the pictures home and compare them to the ones she took. *The* picture of the top of the elevator with the burnt body didn't show the tattoo mark.

If it were on the wall before she fell, that would mean it was part of the graffiti. But, it was not there when the fire investigator did his initial assessment and took this picture. Yet, it

The Fire of Revenge

was there when Marine took her picture last night. That means Ana-Geliza had to put it there sometime after. There is no one else who would do that. The body that was found was not Ana-Geliza—she was alive.

THIRTY-ONE

BOOBY TRAPPED

The house Ana-Geliza and her new partner, the arsonist, had decided to burn was similar in style to the one in which Marine currently lived. It was a Victorian style home with three stories and a full basement, situated just outside the historic district. The fact it was made of brick helped Ana-Geliza convince her comrade to use her signature time-delay. She had perfected it while at TRANS. Marine, if she were any good, would know when she saw it that Ana-Geliza set it. It was her signature.

"Okay. I got the stuff placed 'round the house. It's about four thirty. It will get dark soon. Winter is a great time to burn things, don't you think? It seems a shame to burn this old house when we have that house up the road that is perfectly good and would kill the old woman, too."

"Never you mind about that other house. This is the one we're torching. Now, come here so I can show you about setting the delay. I'll show you, and then I want you to squat down here and do the actual delay. That way I can watch you and make sure you do it correctly. This is one of those delays that will perplex the fire investigators."

"What?"

"They can't figure it out." Ana-Geliza began to demonstrate how to set the delay and as she did, she thought about the time she'd taught Marine how to do it. Back then, she looked up to Marine. She thought they would always be friends. She never guessed that Marine would use her delay to kill her brother. For that, Marine would pay. She would pay dearly.

"Now, here. You do it."

He bent down and began to tilt the small bottle just right with care. He hooked the rubber band that was soaked in gasoline around the neck of the bottle. The other end of the rubber band was nailed to the wall in just the right position.

The Fire of Revenge

Ana-Geliza smiled as she watched him. She made sure that as the rubber band dried, it would contract in the right manner that would cause the bottle to tip, spilling its contents over the igniter of sugar-chlorate setting off the fire. She had timed the delay to give her plenty of time to set the stage and get away.

Right as he finished the setup, Ana-Geliza hit him over the head with the butt of her gun.

"That will teach you to screw with my plans."

She set to work positioning him so that he would burn just enough that Marine would know he didn't set the delay. She placed in his pocket a metal case with clippings of the previous three fires and a piece of paper with a drawing of the tattoo. She took kosher potato chips and dryer sheets, spreading them around and up against the body as well as next to the ignition source. She then took the pile of debris and old clothes they had found earlier lying around the abandoned house and piled it on the body to help it cook.

Ana-Geliza looked around the room, made sure all was set, closed the door behind her, and then walked out to the truck, leaving the time-delay to do its thing. Twenty minutes later, windows exploding out, let the neighborhood know the old house was ablaze. Ana-Geliza drove away as the first fire engine pulled up.

* * * * *

She walked out of the grocery store and placed her bags in the back of her car. The truck pulled up beside her and the driver lowered the driver's side window.

"Excuse me. Could you help me?"

She walked over to the truck, "I'm sorry, I can't hear very well. Do you need something?"

Ana-Geliza got out of the truck. "Could you come back here for a moment? I need some help."

They walked to the back of the truck. Ana-Geliza dropped the tailgate and pointed to the tarp and bag lying there.

"What?"

"I need some help with this. Would you mind helping me?"

As they both leaned forward toward the tarp, Ana-Geliza blew the loose powder of devil's breath into the old woman's face.

It worked quickly.

The Fire of Revenge

Within seconds, the lady responded like a zombie, willingly jumped into the back of the truck, and laid down as instructed, covering herself up with the tarp. Ana-Geliza was pleased how well the drug worked.

The tailgate in place, Ana-Geliza drove away before another person came out of the grocery store.

No one saw her.

THIRTY-TWO

SKYFALL

The moon's light cut through the darkness as the remaining smoke rose up the stairwell. Marine walked up to the bedroom where the fire had started. Earlier, when she did the walk-through with her supervisor, she noticed the time-delay. Then, when they found the metal case, she almost revealed what she knew when she saw the drawing. Ana-Geliza planted that for her, Marine thought as she began to pick around the room. The fire department had put the fire out relatively quick. By the time the fire investigations were finished, it had been two hours since the alarm first went out that there was a blaze here, just blocks away from Aunt Betsy's home. So close. Ana-Geliza was sending a message. But, what kind?

Marine wanted to look at the place alone. She came back a few hours later knowing she would have some privacy. She wanted to make sure she hadn't missed a clue from Ana-Geliza. She couldn't figure out how Ana-Geliza made it out of the other fire alive. And, who was the guy that we found at this one? They might never know.

Marine continued to move around the space. She thought about how the body had been positioned in the first bedroom at the top of the stairs. The fire was contained in the right amount of space to do the least amount of damage to the structure and the body. Ana-Geliza was definitely involved in this.

"You up there?" A voice called.

Marine paused and listened.

"Letsco. I'm here."

Marine stepped carefully from the bedroom doorway. "Do you walk on water, too?"

"I see you still have your sense of humor."

"You're on life number three. Are you like a cat or do you have less lives?"

"Time will tell. I can assure you that *you* don't have long." Ana-Geliza took a step or two and looked up to Marine standing on the landing. "It was a pretty little fire."

"Why are you doing this?"

"Did you find my message?"

"Yes. Who was the guy we found?"

"He was your arsonist."

"Not you?"

"Not for the first three. He let me help him. And he helped me."

"I guess he did since you made it out alive. What gives? What do you want?"

"I want you dead."

"TRANS has folded. You can't expect to have a job with them any longer. Why can't you go on with your own life?"

"You never did listen good. You killed my brother."

"I remember all of my target's names. I never had a target with the last name of Morrison. How did I kill your brother?"

"The time-delay didn't give you a clue?"

Marine flashed back to the fire at the oil refinery. "Your brother was the security guard at the refinery where I used your time-delay setup that you had taught me to use?"

Ana-Geliza nodded. "And you killed him."

"He was a victim of timing. I was almost killed, too. He wasn't supposed to have been at that spot until after the explosion. You can't blame me for that. You've had jobs where things like that have happened."

"I didn't kill your brother."

"Ana-Geliza. You've got to be reasonable about this. You were trained like the rest of us. You were taught to kill and to not think of your victims. I didn't want to kill your brother. I didn't even know he was your brother until now."

"You will know the pain I've suffered."

"I don't have a brother."

"No. No, you don't. But you have people you love. And one of them is with me, now."

Ana-Geliza turned and walked out the door. By the time Marine got down the stairs and out the door, Ana-Geliza was nowhere in sight.

Marine walked back inside the house, picked up her tool kit, and headed to her Jeep. She had to find out whom Ana-Geliza had taken. As she dialed Chet, she figured it was best not to alarm him until she knew that he and Aunt Betsy were safe.

"Hello?"

"Chet, that you?"

"Yes, why?"

"Did I call the wrong number? I'm sorry. I hope I didn't bother you."

The Fire of Revenge

"No, you are fine. Who were you calling?"

"Aunt Betsy. I must've called your cell by mistake. I'll call her."

Marine hung up. Thank God, Chet was okay. Next, she dialed Trout House Falls. The phone rang and rang. Lord, please keep her safe. There was no answer.

At her Jeep, Marine threw her tool kit and bag inside. Someone came walking up behind her with a quick step. The person was in a hooded jacket. Marine turned quickly and got the better of her, thinking it was Ana-Geliza.

"You want to get it on now. Let's do it!"

Marine wrestled with her assailant and managed to knock her down on the ground. "You can't win, Ana-Geliza!"

"Well, that's good, cause I'm not her," Wayne said as Marine recognized him.

THIRTY-THREE

MAYBE YOU'RE RIGHT

They had been sitting in the car about ten minutes as Marine finished bringing Wayne up to speed on the three fatal fires and Ana-Geliza's supposed death and reappearance.

"You realize this could be dangerous for you and your job."

"Yes. That's why I'm telling you. I need an ally; someone I can count on to back me up if things go awry."

"What does Chet know?"

"Nothing about tonight. We need to go tell him. And, then we need to figure out how to find Aunt Betsy."

"Now?"

"Yes. We should have already done it, but you needed to know what was happening." Marine started to get out to go to her Jeep. She turned back to Wayne. "Have you ever had a day that from the moment you opened your eyes you felt like you should have stayed asleep or maybe even died?"

About five minutes later, Wayne and Marine had called Chet back at his apartment. He came right over to Trout House Falls where they explained the night's events.

Chet walked across the room, slammed his fist down on the table. "We have got to find Aunt Betsy. I am going with you. Where do we start?"

"You can't go. We've got to do this following proper procedure."

"Look, Chet, Wayne's right. It's early Friday morning. I'll go with Wayne to the office. We'll see if we can find out any details about the arsonist's family or where he lived."

"No. I have got to go."

Marine walked over to Chet; put her arm around his shoulder. "We need you here in case Aunt Betsy manages to call. Besides, we need one honest soul. If there is anything that I've learned about life and death it is that when you hate, a dark place forms in your soul. And, the universe takes notice. You can't reach the point of hate. That's my job."

"Maybe you are right."

THIRTY-FOUR

SECRETS

Wayne and Marine walked into the fire investigations and bomb squad office.

"I'll go see Chief Fire Marshal Altizer and let him know I'm aware of the work you are doing for me."

Marine smiled at Wayne. "Thank you." She turned and walked over to Tom Willard. "How's it going?"

"We've been working on the leads we found regarding our arsonist. We've managed to make a link to the three fatal fires you worked as a firefighter. Where have you been? The Chief's been looking for you."

"I was at last night's scene. Battalion Chief Foglesong was with me. He's in with the Chief now."

"You working on something on your own?"

"No."

"So what did you find out there?"

"I managed to confirm that there was no additional evidence and that the victim might be a person of interest. Have you gotten anything on him?"

"He's our arsonist."

"How do you know?"

"We received a tip from a concerned citizen less than an hour ago."

Tom handed her the papers collected on the arsonist, Bill Jones, alias Mr. Bill.

"Thanks. I'll sit here and go through these. Do you have anything else?"

"No. Do you?"

"No, not yet."

Marine smiled and started reading through the papers. She began to see several names that kept reappearing. She bet they were family or close friends. If Mr. Bill was helping Ana-Geliza, these people might know where he would have a safe place to hide out or live. She needed to go interview them.

"Tom. I've got a few addresses that I need to check out. I'll be back later."

"What do I tell the Chief?"

"Tell him I'll be back."

The Fire of Revenge

* * * * *

Marine got into her Jeep and drove to the first two addresses.

The first one didn't offer anything that would help. The people were nice and shared they hadn't seen Mr. Bill for at least a year.

The second address, no one was home. Marine was talking to herself about coming up with dead ends when she heard someone call to her.

"Hey, you looking for somebody?"

"Yes. Mr. Bill or Bill Jones."

"He doesn't live here. That's his cousin's place. They're gone for the week. Some kind of trip."

"Okay. Do you know any other family Mr. Bill might have?"

The woman looked suspicious. Marine decided to play a hunch.

"I've got an important paper I need to get to him. It could be valuable to him."

"Did he finally win?"

"Ma'am?"

"The lottery. Did he finally win? He plays all the time. You know, we all do."

"Yes, ma'am. Do you know where I can find him?"

"No."

Marine started to turn.

"But, his sister might."

* * * * *

Marine drove out to the outer edge of the county. She knew that if anyone knew where Mr. Bill's safe place would be, it would be Missy Jones, his sister. She might even know of an old home place or shack in the Jefferson Forest. It was pure luck, the neighbor being such a busybody.

As she drove, she noticed that it was getting darker as the mountain range seemed to grow up out of the ground and the high peaks and trees cut off the late afternoon sun. The road turned from paved to gravel to dirt within a mile. The ruts made driving difficult as Marine tried to steady her phone, note pads, and other items from shifting as the Jeep bounced along.

At one point, the phone fell off the console. She stopped the Jeep, reached down for it and noticed she didn't have any service.

"Great. Just, what I needed. I'm out in the middle of God's country and can't tell anyone."

The Fire of Revenge

An hour later, she pulled up the dirt driveway that led to the old farmhouse back off the rutted road.

"Someone must live here. This driveway is the best road I've been on for a while." She continued on and pulled up next to the broken down barn, which ended at the back door. She walked over to the barn and slid what was left of the old weatherboard aside. No car was inside.

She walked up the back steps and knocked on the screen door.

No answer. No sounds, of any kind.

Marine tried the screen door. It opened. She knocked on the back door.

No answer. No sounds.

She peered through the curtain that hung on the back door window. She could make out what looked like a trail of paper on the floor. She couldn't see much of anything else. She started to walk away when a nagging feeling overcame her. That paper trail looked like it would be a perfect setup to lead a fire to a pile of combustible materials.

Marine stepped back and kicked the door in. She pulled out her gun.

"Hello? Anyone in here? This is Fire Marshal Letsco. I'm with the New Brook Fire Department. Hello?"

Marine walked through the house checking each room using the moves she was taught in the police procedural class and what she knew as an assassin. She froze.

"Aunt Betsy? Aunt Betsy? Can you hear me?" Aunt Betsy was lying on the bed off to the left of the back bedroom. Her feet and hands were tied with what looked like a combustible fuse that was connected to two of several gallon-size glass jars filled with gasoline sitting around the room.

The fuses left the jars and were woven through furniture back to the paper trail. Marine saw bags of nitrate that were wrapped in plastic wrap.

"I bet they were soaked in diesel fuel."

As she walked back, she noticed more glass jars positioned around the house, and more bags of nitrate.

"The house is rigged to blow."

Marine walked back to Aunt Betsy, being careful where she stepped.

"Aunt Betsy? It's Marine. Can you answer me?" Marine was at the doorway, about five feet

The Fire of Revenge

away, studying the setup. Ana-Geliza had apparently rigged Aunt Betsy to the bomb, but Marine wasn't sure at what point she played into the explosion. She hoped that if Aunt Betsy awoke that she wasn't the main trigger.

As she studied what to do next, she holstered her gun and started to walk toward Aunt Betsy.

"I wouldn't go any further if I were you. You'll kill us all."

Marine turned and saw Ana-Geliza standing in the kitchen. She had a gun pointed at her back. Damn, Marine thought. She turned around to face her. "What now?"

"It appears I have you in my sights."

"Funny."

"It is, isn't it?" Ana-Geliza walked toward Marine. "Don't move a muscle. You know I'll shoot. I want your death to last long, but I can end it just as quick as you did for my brother."

Marine looked the room over again to figure out her options. She didn't have many. With Aunt Betsy knocked out or even dead, she didn't have much to help her.

"You're calculating your next moves. You realize you don't have many left."

"Okay. You got me. Get it over with."

"No. I like watching you squirm."

"Let Aunt Betsy go. She hasn't done anything to you."

"You could be right, but you might be wrong. Either way, I'm going to make you suffer. You're going to watch her die." Ana-Geliza took aim at Aunt Betsy.

"Fine. Damn it, we'll all go then." Marine kicked the trip wire and set off a fuse.

She grabbed Aunt Betsy. Jerked the cords from her feet and hands. Drug her into the bathroom throwing her into the claw foot tub, flipping it up and over on them just as the house blew.

The tub rocked back and forth, and Marine could feel the heat. She pushed the tub away and saw the outside walls of the bathroom were gone. The entire house was burning. Aunt Betsy was starting to come around. Marine lifted her up.

"With the walls gone, Aunt Betsy, we're going to go out this way." Marine motioned for her to help her drop to the ground.

Once Marine got Aunt Betsy to the ground and safely away from the burning house, she went to her Jeep where she'd left her phone.

The Fire of Revenge

She dug around in the back and came across her turn out gear.

"Damn. Lot of good this did me out here." She continued to dig and found a bottle of water and a couple of towels. Her left arm was scorched, but not badly. Aunt Betsy, on the other hand, was burned on the left side of her body.

After putting the wet dressing on Aunt Betsy's leg and arm, Marine helped her get into the Jeep.

Aunt Betsy hadn't said a word.

THIRTY-FIVE

FIRE OF REVENGE

That evening after Marine and Aunt Betsy were settled back at Trout House Falls, Chet fixed them one of their favorite treats—Peppermint Patties with homemade ginger snaps.

"Here you go, ladies," Chet said as he carried in the hot cocoa smothered with whipped cream and laced with peppermint schnapps. "Be careful, these ginger snaps might still be a little too warm."

"They smell heavenly," Marine said as she tried to use her burnt arm and realized she needed to use her left one. "I'll be glad when this bandage is gone."

"I am sure you will. The hospital did a good job on both of you. Thankfully, neither of you suffered third-degree burns. How about you, Aunt Betsy? Would you like a cookie?" Chet set her drink down on the side table. Aunt Betsy smiled and shook her head no.

"Aunt Betsy, I am not going to use any psychiatrist tricks on you. I will tell you that I love you."

She smiled and went back to staring out the window into the dark night.

"Marine, see if you can get her to talk to you."

"She will, Chet, when she's ready." Marine took a sip of her drink. "This is delicious." Chet patted Marine on the back and walked back to the kitchen. Marine looked at Aunt Betsy.

"I wish you wouldn't stare at me as though I were dead."

"It speaks."

"Yes, it does." Aunt Betsy tried to reach for her drink and fumbled around. "Damn."

Marine got up and walked over to the side table. She picked it up and repositioned it. "How's that?"

"Thank you."

"No problem. I love you, Aunt Betsy."

"I know."

"Since you don't want to talk much. Do you mind listening to me?"

Aunt Betsy smiled. "Sure. I'll listen. But, first let me say that I wish I could do something kind for you. You have been good to me these last several months, but tonight, Marine, you offered your life for me. That's all I got to say."

Marine bowed her head and wondered how she could share what she needed to say. "I didn't do so great. I failed you in a big way. I wished that I'd been able to kill Ana-Geliza. I had several chances and I blew them. I should have got her. I'm trained. She never should have gotten away."

"You don't know that she did."

"Not officially. The house went quickly, but still. We don't have a body. We don't know for certain."

"Either way, Ana-Geliza will get what she deserves. Evil always does."

"Yes, but I am fearful. You and Chet have done so much for me. I have a chance for a real life here. How can we live knowing she could attack any one of us and we are powerless to stop her? It was pure luck I found you when I did."

Aunt Betsy patted Marine's hand. "It will all work out. Can you trust me?"

Marine smiled. "I guess you are right. You seem to know what I need to hear."

"Marine. Promise me you won't hate her."

"Why? She tried to kill us."

"I know. But, when you hate, you find a dark place in your soul. And, the universe takes notice. We need the universe on our side."

There was a knock at the front door and Marine jumped. "And now, I'm squirrelly. If that's her, I swear."

"No need to worry, Marine. Next time, we won't see her."

Wayne walked into the den with Chet. "I hope you don't mind me dropping by so late, but I thought you'd want to hear the findings of the fire investigation and bomb squad."

"Did you find a body?" Marine asked as she stood to greet Wayne.

"No. There was no body or evidence of a body anywhere in the house. Ana-Geliza is considered armed and a dangerous fugitive. The entire East Coast has been alerted."

"That is something, right?" Chet said as he offered Wayne a drink.

"No thanks, I'm still on duty. But, Marine, I wanted to make sure you both were okay."

"We're fine, Wayne. Thanks."

The Fire of Revenge

"Miss Lanter. Are you doing okay?"

"Yes, Wayne. Thank you."

"Well. That's all I came by for. I wanted to give you the latest news and to see you were doing okay. I'll stop by tomorrow if you like."

Marine stood up and slipped her good arm into Wayne's. "May I walk you out to your car?"

"Sure, but do you feel up to it? It is cold out and I can say good night at the door."

"Okay." Marine turned back and winked at Aunt Betsy.

Chet was gathering up their glass mugs. "Chet, would you help me?" Aunt Betsy rose up from her cozy chair.

"Sure. Where you going?"

"I need to go out to the cottage. I don't think Marine would mind."

"Why? Where are you going to sleep?"

"I'll sleep out there. Marine has two good legs. My left is a little sore and I don't think I should try the stairs."

"How about I help you?"

"No need. I might be banged up a bit, but I'm fine."

"Okay. Do you need anything else?"

"No. I'll be out there a little while. You explain to Marine I'll be out there for tonight, and then you both go on to bed. I'll be fine. You won't need to check on me until morning. The meds the doctor gave me have made me sleepy."

"I hope you will be fine. Are you sure about—"

"I plan on sleeping out in the cottage. That is final. There is a nice bed and bath out there all on one floor. It will make it easier for one night. Now, good night."

"Good night."

* * * * *

Several hours went by and finally the last light in the house went out. Aunt Betsy had dressed using her garden clothes she kept in the back of the garden shed that was behind the cottage. She had managed to get into the garden shed from the cottage using a secret passage she'd created when the cottage was first built.

She grabbed her twenty-two-revolver with its silencer out of its hiding place, and then went back into the cottage. After making sure no one was stirring in the house, she snuck out.

The Fire of Revenge

* * * * *

Just before dawn, Aunt Betsy limped back into the cottage. She closed the door behind her and walked over to Marine's desk. She reached into her pocket. It was still there. After lying down on the bed, she fell asleep.

Later that morning she awoke to Chet shaking her.

"Aunt Betsy? Aunt Betsy, wake up."

"I'm awake. Thank you, Chet."

"Did you sleep in your clothes?"

"Yes. Yes, I did."

"Would you like some breakfast?"

"Yes. I'll go over to the house and up to my room to freshen up. I think I can make it up the stairs. I'm not as sore as I was."

Aunt Betsy climbed the stairs, walked past Marine's door. She stood there and listened. She could hear Marine sleeping soundly. She went into her bedroom, walked over to her dresser.

Sitting on top of the dresser was a nondescript jewelry box. She opened it up and removed the top drawer, reached back into a secret compartment and pulled out a velveteen case about the size of a small book.

As Aunt Betsy opened the case, she simultaneously pulled out a lock of long, ebony hair from her pocket.

She carefully placed the lock of hair into the case.

"No one messes with my family, especially my granddaughter."

Plan to return and visit with Marine in Book Three of The Marine Letsco Trilogy

A TIME FOR FIRE

What fire investigations will Marine pursue? Does Marine's future include a relationship with Drake? What happens to her friendship with Wayne? Who is Aunt Betsy? How does Chet fit into Marine's plans? Look for the concluding story of Marine Letsco in the forthcoming novel, *A Time for Fire* available in print and eBook format.

VISIT

PAM B. NEWBERRY

at her website:

http://pambnewberry.com

Learn how to become a Happy V. I. P. Reader.

ACKNOWLEDGEMENTS

After writing book two of this trilogy, I can still say that asking readers to take a chance at reading my words is still hard. The rewards of writing this second novel have come at unlikely times—when doing research or asking questions or meeting someone who has read book one—*The Fire Within*. The joy comes when I see the gleam in a reader's eyes and she asks—"How's writing book two coming along?" Or, he says, "I can't wait to read it." I hope you find this second installment as much fun to read as I had writing it for you.

My husband, Albert, continued his role as supporter—faithfully pointing out I needed to fix dinner or wash clothes. Once, he even helped me write a chapter. He is my soulmate and gives me a reason to laugh when my muse flies away. Thank you, with all of my heart. I love you, always.

Julie, our daughter, and her dog, Miloh, are not only my loyal supporters, but provide me with joy when writing zaps it out of me. Again, Julie, you have worked magic with the book cover. You have that knack to pinpoint what I want to see. I love you, dearly.

A writing friend and editor that I've come to rely on relentlessly—Rosa Lee Jude—has given me multitudes of advice, and I've listened to each one. Thank you.

The beta readers—Connie Martin, Marcella Taylor, and Carole Bybee—provided suggestions that were of high merit and went far beyond what I had hoped for, and I am grateful!

To Donna Stroupe—a reader with an eagle eye bar none—Thank you for helping to improve my story.

To my friends and friends to be, thank you for being readers of my words. Moreover, thank you for writing and connecting with me to let me know if I've touched your life in some small way.

There are so many more who offer support, please know I thank you very much.

Write on!

ABOUT THE AUTHOR

Pam B. Newberry lives in the mountains of Southwest Virginia with her husband where she is at work on her next book. The author of the Marine Letsco Trilogy and *The Letter: A Page of My Life*, she enjoys fun in the sun.

Connect with Pam through her website:
http://pambnewberry.com.

Made in the USA
Charleston, SC
21 October 2015